W.A.Harbinson is the author of two bestselling novels, *Genesis* (1980) and *Revelation* (1982). His epic fictional series, 'Projekt Saucer', including *Inception, Phoenix, Genesis, Millennium,* and *Resurrection,* remained in print for most of the 1990s. An updated edition of Harbinson's seminal nonfiction work, *Projekt UFO: The Case for Man-Made Flying Saucers* (1995) was published as a POD book in 2008. A science-fiction novelette, *Into The World of Might Be*, was also published as a POD book in 2008.

Web Site: www.waharbinson.eu.com

Knock

W.A.Harbinson

Custom Books Publishing

First published by Intergroup Publishing, London, in 1975
This edition published in 2009 by W.A.Harbinson

www.waharbinson.eu.com

ISBN: 1448657237
EAN-13: 9781448657230

Designed on the Isle of Wight , Great Britain, by www.inkdigital.org

For Ursula, Shaun and Tanya

W.A. Harbinson
Foreword

Readers familiar with my more commercial fiction should be warned that *Knock* is a very different kettle of fish. It is, in fact, a 'literary' novel, slightly *avant garde*, of the kind that many friends felt I should have continued to write, rather than the more mainstream novels that later made up the bulk of my career. It is therefore being republished purely for nostalgic reasons and because, despite a few reservations, it still holds a warm place in this author's heart. A few words regarding how it came about would not be remiss.

In 1975, when I was living in London, a good friend and professional art director, Miles Walker, rang me to say that he was working for a new, independent publishing company, Intergroup, that had been successfully publishing poetry and books of philosophy, but now wanted to try some literary fiction. To this end, he asked me if I would be willing to write an original 'literary' novel for Intergroup. I agreed to try and do so. I would receive no advance, but I would be paid the standard royalties on all copies sold. Four weeks later I completed a full-length novel, *Knock*.

Inspired by the prose style of J.P. Donleavy (whose *The Ginger Man* and *A Singular Man* were two of my favourite comic novels), *Knock* was a comic tragedy about the last week in the life of a London postman, known only as 'Postie', who is dying of chronic bronchitis but doesn't know it. The stream-of-consciousness narrative was, however, broken up with a few surrealistic dream sequences that made liberal use of the kind of dreams I was having at the time, which was a troubled time in my life. To the main text was added a perhaps too generous foreword by Colin Wilson, best-selling author of *The Outsider* and many other books. That foreword has been reprinted as an afterword to this new edition of *Knock*.

A few hundred copies of *Knock*, produced as a trade paperback, were bound and sent out to reviewers and a few

London bookshops, but Intergroup folded before any more copies could be printed; thus, *Knock* was seemingly lost for good. It did, however, receive at least two serious reviews, one of which contradicted the other.

Reviewing the novel for *The Guardian*, Robert Nye opened his assassination attempt by pointing out to his readers that the author of *Knock* was a 'one-time plumber, now the Chief Associate Editor of *Men Only*, and author of books about Elvis Presley, Sammy Davis Jr., and Marlon Brando.' (I had, by that time, written a bestseller biography of Elvis, but only articles about Davis and Brando.) Having thus set me up as a hopeless case, Nye then sneered at Colin Wilson's 'extraordinary' introduction, demolished the novel ('its only spark of interest lying in the distance between the randy randomness of the postman's thoughts and the precision of his way of speaking'), and climaxed by returning to his opening put-down with the suggestion that 'Mr Harbinson may be better at his show-business activities.'

Michael Maxwell Scott, on the other hand, writing in the *Daily Telegraph*, said of the same novel: 'The stream-of-consciousness technique is a tricky one, apt to slump into self-consciousness, but W. A. Harbinson handles it like a virtuoso... A very Irish figure, this literary postman. He belongs really to the streets of Joycean Dublin – or perhaps Mr Harbinson's Belfast – not London. So do most of the other figures in this sad, moving, often beautifully funny and engagingly stately progress through a man's mind and past.'

Reviewers can kill a writer as they almost certainly did the American World War II novelist, John Horne Burns, who committed suicide after receiving dreadful reviews for his third novel. They did not kill me. I was, however, lucky. If the *Guardian* review had been the only one I received, it is possible that I would have been so devastated that I would never have written again. In the event, because I received such a sterling review that same week in the *Daily Telegraph*, I was able to calmly compare one to the other and deduce that objective judgement was hardly to be expected from critics. Thereafter, I would not be wildly bothered by them, though undeniably preferring good reviews to bad.

Here, then, is a new edition of *Knock*, doomed by a blighted birth, but resurrected, hopefully still alive and well, after all these years.

W. A. Harbinson
West Cork, Ireland
2009

Knock

Prologue

Eternal sun mocked the passing of this fugitive, ephemeral life. The curtains shivered and the light expanded, illuminating motes of dust at play. The people outside were curious; those inside, briefly stricken. A throttled moan from the man on the couch, an anguished wail from the girl by his side. There was the metallic click of a medical bag, shut by professional fingers. Somewhere a sports car roared. And nothing stood still.

 -Too late!

 -No!

This wail of despair was remotely heard by the man who lay on the couch. He was dying. The light in the blue of his eyes was quickly receding. And tears which fell on his postman's uniform were mistaken for shining rivers. He smiled exposing healthy teeth which considering his age was a miracle. There was a hint of silver in his hair, his face had been corrugated by the elements, but he did not look his late middle-age. Those outside were growing restless, but the man was indifferent. His family was missing, the girl's tears were flowing, and nobody in the room knew his name.

 -Doctor! He's choking!

 -Postman, Postman, bring me...

The doctor initialled various government forms while the man on the couch continued dying. Little else could be done. The days were long and filled with crises, life and death being treated as equals. It was a clear-cut case of acute bronchitis and should have been treated a week ago. At the least. And this one an ageless man. No name. The street's residents simply knew him as 'the Postman'.

Either he had known and hadn't cared or was as tough as nails or just mad. There were usually clear symptoms. His family should have noticed. Erratic speech, explosive temper, with perhaps a dash of paranoid suspicions. Not forgetting a strengthened libido. He, or they, should have noticed.

Symptoms.

Now, too late. Ring the post office, obtain his area code, and from that they could ascertain his name. Such being modern society. Organised. But the doctor neatly gathered in his papers.

-A wonder he didn't realise.

-Beware, beware, the Postman's knock.

The girl laced her fingers across her face and wept the tears of a child. She had thought about death, sometimes knowing it in dreams, and at last it had come to her own door. This charming old man with the quick-silver tongue, now going with no family to grieve him. Only yesterday smiling, yet now choking his lonely way to the grave.

Had he sensed it at all? Had she *not looked close enough? He had been dying, dying all that last week and no-one had remotely realised.*

Oh, Lord, the shame! Dear God, the horror! How could he be going before her very eyes with afternoon sunlight on his face? His hair was streaked with silver, his bright eyes turning dark, his smile at once benign and unsuspecting. What had he thought? What had he felt? How had he actually lived that final week?

The girl wept as the armies of pain tramped over her stricken heart.

Chapter One

The postman's knock. And no filthy remarks. On the door.
Knock-knock. Waiting for the shiver of dusty curtains and one
large, terrified eye. She always does it. Same time every
morning. Knows damned well who it is but looks anyway.
Terrified of sleeping, more terrified of waking up, middle-aged,
unmarried and doubtless sex-mad. Should accept her invitation.
Some sweet day. Step inside, speak words of love, and then try
to make real my own hopeful dreams. But wouldn't dare. The
hysteria would break me down. And her claws once in never out.
Frustrated spinsters, invitations to tea, and bang goes my nice
easy job. The only job more precarious than a meter maid's is a
postman's. I should know, being nobly of the latter breed.

The curtains shiver and so do I. Between curtain-gloom and
window-frame, one large, nervous eye. Miss Eleanor Rigby. A
tender, fragile soul. Scared witless by the knowledge that she's
alive. Reading romance novels and the Holy Bible and living her
minutes for the Postman's knock. Receiver of mysterious
registered parcels. From loved ones afraid to approach? Or
relatives who want her dead? And deary me, but who knows?

Shiver go the curtains and away goes that eye. Dear Miss
Rigby. Thrilled and embarrassed because a mop-haired singing
group used her name in a sad song. Secretly in love with Archie
Brown. The neighbour across the road. A six-foot ditch-digger
from Deal. Who makes weekly trips to Old Compton Street and
returns smelling of booze and cheap whore's flesh. Every
Sunday morning. Always shortly after midnight. Comes along

this dark street made bright by the lamplight. Vomiting stumbling and scratching at his balls. With a sweet if you see kay for everyone. And poor Eleanor Rigby. Most secretly and romantically in love with him.

Pitiful. And her front door always opens, creaking as it yawns, letting light escape from her prison to fall on the paving stones.

-Morning, Miss Rigby. And a fine one it is, too. Sun shining. Air fit for human consumption. Step outside and be warmed. Before it all goes again, my beauty.

A few cheerful words. Not forgetting the little compliment. Does her the power of good and doesn't cost much. Slight blush on her cheeks and a stifled titter of mirth. Pale fingers like a web at her cheeks.

-Oh, you!

-Oh, me!

-Oh, my!

We play this little game every time I deliver mail. Which makes the teeth grind. Given the childishness of it all. But stout civil servant, devoted lackey to Queen and Country, doing one's duty to those one serves. And God rest her soul, but she could do with the encouragement. Though with a figure like that she should have had it years ago. On a regular basis.

A nice wee drop in its fashion. And a mystery why it's never been sampled. Or has it? You can never really tell. The Rigby bed might have taken more poundings than those to which Archie Brown runs every Saturday evening. And what a lewd thought in the presence of such a lady. Even if tantalising.

-Miss Rigby. If I may be so bold. You're a sight worth sampling to these weary old eyes.

-Oh, Mister Postman, you shouldn't *say* such things.

Turning away slightly. Blushing but pleased. Dressed in grey to match the pavements. For instant invisibility. Yet really very attractive. Even counting in the face. Pale, plain and pained. Otherwise almost pretty. Plus hints of sensuality in the mournful eyes. Which blinking are reflecting the morning light.

Ah, Lord, but what a shame. A ripe piece like that going to waste and frustration. And here's me tied to a well-meaning pudding with an addiction to cheese sandwiches and chips. Fine farting food. Not refined like Miss Rigby. Now brushing back auburn hair with trembling fine-boned fingers. Raising the large dark orbs to express fluttering yearning and dread.

-You have... something... for me?

-Trust the postman's knock, Miss Rigby. Yours and yours alone. Presentation herewith.

Red wax on brown paper. Sealed, stamped and registered. To bring hope for another horrid day. Her torture temporarily eased. Making her sigh. Hugging the package to her tits. Glancing at the sender's name. With a grateful sigh disguising her despair.

-Oh, *thank* you. What it must be to be a... *postman*. So... *gratifying*.

Turning away. Blushing with embarrassment. Lovely line to the swan's neck. Breath coming hard and nervous. *You're such a kind man.* And: *A cup of tea, perhaps?* Always know exactly what's coming.

-You're such a kind man. A cup of–

-Love to, Miss Rigby, but duty calls, as you know. Others await me and I never drink, ha, ha, during working hours.

-Tea.

-No. Not even that.

She signs the receipt, pen quivering over the receipt-book, paper rustling like her dress as she recedes back into that small gloom. Click. Goes the door. As gentle as she is. Then more silence in this early morning street.

The pearly light on faded brick. Bending lines of broken pavements. Already warming underfoot. A quiet, anonymous street. But interesting behind the curtains. A thought tempting one to knock there again. To slip inside for tea. And anything else she may be offering. Loins melting at the thought of it.

17

Which is not really surprising. Being right sprightly for this ripe old age. Cornflakes, of course. Giving nourishment to the body. And clarity to the brain. Encouraging contemplation and subsequent searching questions. Such as who sends the gifts? No one darkens that door but her own lonely self. Who cares enough to buy wrap and register the packages? Could find out by simply asking. But naturally don't do it. Being sensitive to esoteric sensibilities. Though some day might weaken and make indirect enquiries. Meanwhile. Every day the postman calls is Christmas Day. Minus the tips.

We need the gratitude. All of us. The last of the Good Samaritans. With a touch of the masochistic. Canvas bag on the shoulder. Chafing skin and bruising bone. While dragging us down. Toward the pavements and weariness. The bag being heavy. With paper hopes and dreams. Entreaties and threats and words of love and hatred. Tales of joy and sorrow and triumph and defeat. The envelopes reeking. Of piss and powder. Shit and scent. What we are and what we use to disguise it when the truth becomes evident.

-Morning, Madam!

-Hmph!

Tip the peaked cap. At this crotchety old bag passing tight-lipped. Smile politely. At her wealth of baseless malice. Foul witch. The bitch. Built like a barn, about as graceless as a gorilla, and with a face like a lump of mouldy cheese. Despises the world and everyone in it. Thrives on the humiliation of others. And brings up her offspring accordingly. Horrible little monsters. Always covered in filth and foul-mouthed. Throwing firecrackers through Miss Rigby's mailbox when darkness has fallen.

-Goodbye, Madam!

-Hmph!

But don't forget the smile. Obscene gesture only when she's passed by. Meanwhile. Keep walking. With the amplifiers pinned back and the perceptive orbs open. This street just one of many but enough to be getting on with. Lots to see. Lots to hear. This job actually quite interesting. At times. Assuming you don't mind the flat feet and bent back. The sun, wind, rain, frost, snow and falling birdshit. Now the Dragon Lady, Whittaker, also known as Pig Features, has passed and walked on a safe distance. So make with the promised obscene gesture. Too late. One of her brats has seen what we have done and is spreading the word.

-I saw ya! I saw ya!

An undernourished Lolita presently covered in grime. Would seem more presentable if locked in a cage. Now jumping energetically. Up and down on the pavement. Flashing tattered knickers and pointing a grubby accusing finger. Would like to wring her scrawny neck. But instead vigorously swing this canvas bag. At her tender head.

Thud. A scream. Into the gutter where she belongs. Howling histrionically and yelling for her Mum. Who returns on the instant. Further damaging the paving stones. Bloated with anger and blind self-esteem. Hands on fat hips staring nastily.

-An accident, Madam, I assure you. Collision as one sees on the frantic roads. The child ran straight out of the house and inadvertently into my mailbag. I implore you. Note the dent in the canvas.

Inadvertently. An impressive word, to be sure. From the enormous dictionary from a quick-talking salesmen. Who robbed me wicked one sunny afternoon when my defences were down. But now worth the price for the look of stupefaction on her slack-jawed Neanderthal face. As well as the introduction to even more sarcastic lingo. At which I am most adept. A fact she soon appreciates when she opens her mouth. To offer me abuse. Four-lettered and foul. Which I do not take lightly as I look her in the eye. And prepare to stand cool and dignified.

-He hit me, Mum! That old bastard hit me! Banged me head with that bag of his!

Squalid little brat. Ought to slap her up and down the street.

To teach her some manners. Better still. Tie her in my bag and drop it into the River Thames. Stand on Battersea Bridge to observe the rising bubbles. All foaming and silvery-white. On that scum-dappled deep. Saving some future local council from taking expensive legal action. Against her future adult iniquities. Taxpayers grateful. Along with the mothers of respectable young gentlemen. Who would shudder if they knew that she was waiting for them in the more dangerous, adolescent years. In the uncomfortably close future.

Reality is what it is. Which is more than enough. So eye to eye with the awful mother. Concentrate on breathing evenly and keeping one's cool. While she vomits up her slanderous words.

-Fuckin' vicious brute in yer fascist uniform! Pickin' on childern and helpless wimmen. I'll report ya, mark m'words. To the proper authorities. Have ya out of a job and back in the dole queue wonderin' where yer next penny's comin' from. Attackin' an innocent child for no good reason. Perverted old bastard that ya are! I'll have ya wankin' in Pentonville prison for the rest of yer life!

-The child, Madam, is lying. Possibly hysterical. Believe me, I hold no grudge.

-Sure I'd write to the GPO but what good would it do? They'd probably tell me the letter got lost in one of their stupid sortin' machines. Either that or they'd go on bloody strike again. Payin' taxes to support all them lazy commie cunts and a horde of child-molesters like yerself. Somethin' should be done about it but what can a body do? Just write to the newspapers, liars the lot of 'em, and get not a word back in reply. Aren't ya all in the same gang, the fuckin' lot of ya?

And so on and so forth. Almost foaming at the mouth. Further words unprintable and gestures beyond description. But eventually grabs her brat, tries to drag her away, finds resistance and belts her around the ears with truly admirable vigour. Childish shrieks. Motherly screams. Then back into their pigstye of a house. Two riot-creating swine in human disguise. Not quite the pride of the street but certainly making their mark here.

Two doors farther along. Dropping a letter into the cleaner house of Mr and Mrs Bleakley. A decent Christian pair being driven to despair by the behaviour of their daughter Louise. The letter is one of love to Louise from a delinquent boyfriend in Hornsey. Across the back of it, possibly scrawled in blood, the letters S.W.A.L.K. Sealed with a loving kiss. And vile intentions.

Louise is sixteen, sexy and obliging. Once confided that she liked doing it in cramped places. Such as telephone booths. Standing legs apart pierced by you know what. A shocking disclosure. Which made me want to spank her. Where it would be nice to do so. But remembered my age and stood back from temptation. I'm older then Miss Rigby and feeling the pinch. A sad state of affairs but unavoidable.

A tragic day when my first girlfriend stood in white. Looking much plumper than a virgin bride should. And her parents despising me for being no more than a postman. A mere twenty-four years ago. Twice my youth, God help me. And still I have designs on Miss Rigby.

-Postman, Postman, bring me an aerogramme.

Standing in her doorway wearing blue denims and tight sweater. The delightful Mrs Mary McKay. Nineteen years old and only six months married. Her husband a soldier in Belfast. He ducks the bombs while she dreams of babies and waits for his safe return home. Never personally believed in love, but she makes me feel mistaken. Auburn hair over dark-chocolate eyes. A flush on alabaster cheeks. Smile radiant as she leans out of the doorway to deliberately stare at my mailbag. I adore her. Secretly. And every morning, before starting on my rounds, look into the bag and hope with her.

-Postman, Postman, bring me an aerogramme.

She will not accept defeat. And is rewarded every two or three days. And always presses the letter to her lips, as she does right now.

-Joe, you're a wonderful man.

-My name isn't Joe.

-You always say that but I don't believe you. And I *like* you as Joe.

-I like you as you.

-You're a dear man to say that.

-I only say it to young ladies in love with other men.

Leaning back against the doorframe, legs crossed, body languid. Licking the envelope with a loving tongue. Chocolate eyes almost melting. Making me feel an immeasurable loss. Which I cannot remotely understand. Let alone accept.

-I told him about you. I wrote and told him that we had the most wonderful postman in London. He wrote back to ask if I had fallen in love with you. Just a little bit, I told him. Our Postie is a gentle, fatherly man. That's what I wrote. Is it true?

-I'm not gentle, I'm tired. I'm not fatherly, I'm old.

-I hope Michael grows old like you.

-Go in and read your letter, Miss Lovelorn.

-Oh, yes, I'll do that, alright.

Smiles with a touch of heaven and then she's gone. Back to her paper husband. To warmly cherished, recent memories. Perhaps back to the kind of feelings I have not known and now simply don't want to know.

Ah, truly I grow old. Deep lines in the face and cynicism in the soul. Now crossing the road. To the house of the widow Peggy Hartnett. With whom I lie in the evenings when I'm supposed to be at the pub. Beer, sex and the sports I can't play all observed on a television screen. A pleasant social life. Modest enough, but sustaining. I dare not speak to Peggy in the exposing light of day but slip miscellaneous items through her mailbox. Advertising leaflets, magazines, bills, invoices, and regular letters of complaint from the mother who hibernates in Bournmouth. Fading away with each sunset.

But move briskly on. To find Archie Brown groping bedraggled on his doorstep for his morning milk. Eyes bloody, hands trembling. Hair dishevelled and chin dark with stubble.

Not the most glorious sight. At this hour of the morning.

-If it's a bill, I don't want it.

-I must deliver. After that, it's up to you.

-Conscientious bastard, aren't you?

-A man must perform his duty.

-Oh Christ, oh Jesus, my aching back!

Manages to grab the bottle and stand upright again. Rising painfully and shakily one immense crumbling man. Reeking of stale ale, unsavoury living and onion bajees. A radio crackling behind him inside his gloomy house. A distorted male voice discussing losses and gains in fun-filled Belfast. While Archie sways there, free hand searching for the doorframe. Streaks of red in the eyeballs which blinking start weeping. Thus paying for his sins before starting all over again. Two cans of lager in the fridge to set him right for the new day. Last night a brawl and one swollen blue cheek. Justice will out.

-Here, Archie. Your latest bill. Please take it.

-I can't pay it. Christ, my head!

-You can't pay it because you're spending all your money on drink.

-Not my fault, mate. I'm suffering from stress. In America, I'd be seeing a psychiatrist, but here I can only drink.

-And the swollen blue cheek?

-Not my fault either. Just another unfortunate incident. This sod came straight at me bawling down with Labour and up all them slimy-faced Tories. So I let the bastard have it between the tonsils and down he went like an anchor. But then got up again. And let me have it where you see it. So this time it was me who went down. And I didn't get up again. Instead woke up in the gutter. Minus wallet and optimism. And think I'm now feeling the pinch, if you can manage to grasp that.

-Pardon?

-Electricity cut off, fridge therefore not working, and canned lager foaming out like warm piss. Oh, boy, can a man win?

-I fear not.

-How right you are.

Disappears. With a crash, bang and tumble. Over the furniture. Before cursing distinctly. Followed by distant squeaking as the fridge door is opened. Another day beginning with a man talking casually. About violence on both sides of the Irish Sea and elsewhere. War, rape, unsolved murders and genocide. Though the sun still shines. Over cracked peaceful pavements. Ants industrious in the cracks. The bleak rows of terraced houses with backyards lacking gardens. And far off the sound of a train and city traffic. Reverberating even here at the house of Hans Wernher. A refugee from Belsen. Where the doctors attempted some unorthodox experiments and permanently stunted his proper growth. Leaving him as a wretched malformed creature. Perverted by hatred.

Once stepped tentatively inside to check out his hovel. Stale bread on the table, sour milk on the floor and unwashed clothing in the sink. Death and decay almost palpable in the air, yet Wernher would clearly live to be a hundred. Handed me a cup begrimed with phlegm and sneeringly offered some cold tea. Which I politely refused. Too many memories of childhood poverty and parents dying choking in the night. Such being life's rich reward. And so, here and now, the awkwardly bent Hans Wernher. Squinting upward through sunlight with his crooked grin malicious. And oral diarrhoea on his tongue.

-What's worse? A philosopher with a bent spine or a postman with flat feet?

Deformed bodies I can tolerate but deformed minds disturb me. Has he enjoyed the company of anyone since those days and nights of singular torture? It's doubtful. Yet I pity him. While wanting to peel the flesh from his miserable bones, layer by layer. See what goes on inside him. What makes him tick. The thought of which curdles the blood. And also encourages mischief. It being that one is rarely without the irresistible urge. To plant one's firm boot in his mocking Kraut mug. Making him

24

feel something, if only that.

Instead. Hand him this latest letter. German stamp. And watch him throwing it over his misshapen shoulder. As he does with every letter he receives.

-They keep pretending. My parents. Pious words of love scribbled routinely on cheap paper. Scented with mother's sweet lies. Come home, come home, they implore repeatedly. Stop living like a schlemiel. They quote me two-thousand years of victimisation and expect blood to be thicker than water. Which, in this particular case, it is not. When the Nazis released me I crawled like a crab and my parents were ashamed and sent me here. Now they are old and self-pitying, needing someone to care for them. I only reply in order to spit upon them. Would you care to join me over a cup of urine?

-I never drink before lunch.

-The postman is a wit. This I appreciate. But you should save it for more appropriate occasions, perhaps writing it down for posterity. More likely, though, it would serve as entertaining graffiti on the walls of a public shithouse. So it may be wiser to remain as a postman. Flat feet and empty brain. Ah, ha! I offend you and make you want to hit me. Go on! Pick on a man half your size. And with terrible handicaps.

-You're an offensive swine not worth hitting.

-Insults from a civil-servant. I could have you hung, drawn and quartered, but won't. Indolence prevents me from writing to those who employ you and thank your lucky stars it is so. Still, I note that the widow Hartnett is looking younger every day, so perhaps you are doing some good there. The only thing more corruptible than a crippled philosopher is a woman lacking child or cuckoldry. The child she can do without, but the cuckoldry she needs. Trust our postman to make such philanthropical visits by night.

Start walking and don't look back. The only way to treat the disgusting creature. Which nonetheless leaves the urge to make amends. Pornographic snapshots through his mailbox. That should do the trick. The prick has never had it in his miserable life and the sight of such items should scald him. Think of the insult, if nothing else. Take pleasure in imagining the scene. Moaning in his soiled sheets and jerking off on his squalid bog. Frustration has its limits and that would be his. So must keep this in mind the next time foxy Wilson starts passing around his obscene Asian souvenirs. A quid for six black and whites. A cheap price to pay to keep Wernher awake at night. Though what low thoughts to be thinking this otherwise pleasant day.

-Good day to you, sir!

That's it. Tip the peaked cap to the man collecting life-insurance payments. A slim soul. Shy. Ashamed of his profession. Of his vampire tendencies. The blood-sucker.

-Morning, Madam!

And keep walking. Before you get a mouthful of troubles not your own. As if your own weren't enough to be going on with. Which they are, to be sure.

Better warn the widow Hartnett to be more careful. The scandalous word is being passed on. Which could ruin one. Especially with the wife. Who is intolerable but cooks the meals. And the meals of course making life worth living when all else is misery.

Mailbag chafing the shoulder. Feet becoming hot. As well as hurting from the corns. Perhaps some day they'll amputate and give me metal replacements. Which would make me a more modern man than I am at this moment.

Now in front of number thirty-seven. Two lean young men in purple tracksuits in the sunlight. Flushed and sweating. Twins. Always keen on fast cars and even faster ladies. Now performing rigorous push-ups. On the pavement. To the disgust of passers-by. Talking all the while. While nostalgia comes from watching their youthful agility. And from the knowledge that only in the presence of the young does one feel old.

-Hi, Postie! What've you got for us today?

-Motor magazines, sex magazines, various bills and call-up

papers.

-Man, you kill us. You really do. National Service, no less. This is now a free country, Granddad. The bad old days are gone.

Daniel or David talking. I can't tell one from the other. They look so much alike. And appear to like each other. Which might or might not be a good thing. Since time parts us all from brothers and other loved ones. Cruelly depriving us of those we most need. And use for support. Though the twins don't need that. Being healthy and self-sufficient. Fair hair flopping over faces well preserved by modern vaccines. Eyes bright and enthusiastic. Though for what I often wonder. Since. At their age it wasn't concrete pavements. Upon which I practised my push-ups. So suspect a dubious relationship here. But put the suspicions down to middle-aged envy. Dwelling on what evil thoughts we secretly harbour for others. If also intriguing and keeping the mind engaged. While their bronzed sweat-slicked skin makes me yearn for a cold beer. Lunchtime now being not too far off. And today being Saturday I long for it even more. As the lads jump to their feet. To spar jokingly on the pavement. Showing off for the benefit of admiring eyes. Including those of young girls unencumbered by inhibitions. Thus offering some hope. With which to cleanse the filthier thoughts of this suspicious postman.

-Hey, Postie. How's you getting on with Tina Louise?

A little discretion at this point. Feign innocence. Bland face for the defeat of such naughty enquiries.

-*Whom*?

-Tina Louise. That teenage sex-pot. Tight skirts and big knockers. Teasing us healthy athletes into a lather.

-Oh, you mean *Louise*!

-Oh, man, what an actor you are. But don't think we haven't been watching you. You cunning old dog. Smiling almost foaming at the mouth. Patting her bare shoulder as if it doesn't mean a thing. While your knees are visibly shaking. With more than the weight of that mailbag. Lecher! Sex fiend! We see all the signs. You're working your way quietly toward Hyde Park in the evenings, an incompetent rape, and the lurid front pages of the Sunday rags. Not that we mind. I mean, we're tolerant guys. And we think you're the most interesting pervert that the street has to offer. But have a heart, Postie. Give we adolescents a break. Reserve your worldly wisdom and experience for some older bags. And leave that poor kid alone.

-Gentlemen, you wrong both me and sweet Louise.

-All right. Okay. You win. Throw the mail in the hallway and go about your business. We like you, but the competition frightens us. Though some day we'll get in there, Postie. Don't worry about *that*. We have to. It's for the good of the species. So keep your paws in your pockets.

-Forgive an old man his indiscretions.

And getting off these words off we go along the street. Invigorated by the contact. Since, in our own fashion, we sincerely like the lively lads. Definitely not virgins but virtuous all the same. Best of the best. Hope of the future. Stout hearts, tingling balls, and no thoughts about dying. For their country or anything else. There being not an ounce of patriotism between them. Just youth. And vitality. Something I lack at this moment. The sun being out in full strength. And sweat beginning to run. With the mailbag becoming lighter and the feet feeling heavier. And the hint of a cough coming on.

Curse these old lungs. Always protesting. Driving one to drink, furtive sex and unpleasant tantrums. Which makes for the sanity. If such there be. Thanking God, as one does now and then, that there are only two streets left on the beat. After which another week's work will end. To be followed by a pub-lunch with boozy companions. Both necessary evils. With which to combat the quiet hell of a domestic afternoon. Spent with the wife, don't you know.

So it goes and so it is. Though would end it if I could. Since would never have married had it not been for accidental encounters. And premature swellings. Remorse tinged with pride for such was youth. Thus joined in wedlock and suffered for life. Tied to a nagging shrew and demanding offspring. Which just goes to prove. Alas, too late. That a man must always look before he leaps.

Now sweating like a pig. The head filled with lewd fantasies. Seeing cracked pavements as so many miles while female flesh unpeels before me in the mind's darkened bedroom. Yet still in this same street. My favourite thoroughfare. So lost in thoughts of a shameless sexual nature that I almost trip over Pete Whelan's chair. Then actually stumble into it. Making him fall cursing to the ground. Before hastily righting himself.

-Shit, Postie, are you blind?

-A thousand pardons, Pete.

-Almost knocked me out of me chair.

-I succeeded.

-And doubtless feel satisfied.

Fine lines of age around this one's grey eyes. The skin of his face red and wrinkled. Thinning hair neat, cigarette splitting lips, grinning crookedly, wickedly. Fought at Dunkirk, damned near died, never mentions it. A rare breed. Certainly. Indeed, almost archaic. Coughing flecks of dark-crimson blood into a white handkerchief.

-Don't tell me, Postie. You've brought me nothing again. Worthless as the day is long, you are. If only for the present. But some day you'll bring me that money I dream about. I refuse to give up. My win on the pools will occur before these lungs cough their last. Then it's a cruise around the world. For myself and the missus. As a reward for all we've endured together without too much bile. The postman's just got to bring the good news, which one fine day he will. Or be damned for his failure.

And laughs. At himself. Until the laughter degenerates into painful coughing. And the handkerchief comes out again. Crimson flecks on white cloth. Though his smile still radiates optimism. And defies death's advance.

A few modest pleasantries. Grinning back at his grin.

Offering a saucy joke while taking note of the gay lines around his grey eyes. Hiding thoughts of that crimson soaking into the white cloth. And of ocean voyages that he hopes will be made with the wife now hiding upstairs. So wave and walk away. Faster from the doomed. Toward the end of this English summer street and imminent freedom.

Two more streets to go. But this one the only real one. Each of the others a world unto itself, self-contained, multifaceted. All thriving on hope. And despair and joy and grief. All filled with local conflict and gossip and intrigues. But this one my own, my favourite street.

A street of dreams and redemption.

Now hot. The sun fierce. Silvery light in the eyes. Body throbbing with familiar aches and pains. The mind filled with thoughts of pleasures. Cold beer and warm friends and love awaiting the evening's coming darkness. A short distance to go. In the next couple of minutes. Then walk out of this street. And out of another week. The postman's knock. Knock, knock on the doors.

Temporarily silenced.

Chapter Two

-Well, lookahere! The Postie! Public Servant Number One.

-Bill. Frank. Marge. How are you?

-All rightey. How's yourself?

-A wearied soul. But content. At peace, as it were.

-What'll it be, Postie?

-A pint of bitter, nicely drawn.

-Anything exciting happen, Postie? Bitten by any mad dogs? Raped by any licentious women? Beaten up by any rampaging adolescents?

-A quiet day. Uneventful. Almost soothing.

-Your beer, Postie.

-Thank you, Marge. And I think I'll have a sausage. With a little hot sauce. To encourage the beer on its journey.

-Gee, I love the way you talk. Such a gentleman to be only a postman.

Tits. Two of them. Pressed against the cash-register. Taut as two Lambeg drums. Lovely grub. Would rather chew on them than on sausage with sauce. And what a saucy thought that is. Unmitigated horror. If she could read my pagan mind. Not that I'm to blame. With her displaying them like that. In the half-unbuttoned blouse. Right under a man's nose. It really shouldn't be allowed. Though a curse on the man or woman who would ban it. Since truth be known I'm all for it. Trapped as I am in the deep pit of matrimony. Which makes a man. Require some alternate sexual outlet. Even if only in the thoughts. So today a few wee drinkies. Tonight a little hanky-panky. Intervening period more bearable if ignored. More sensible to dwell on that row of shiny bottles. Along the back of the bar. And the glasses of amber liquid. Always good for the calories. Otherwise would avoid them. And what a vile lie that has to be in the eyes of the Lord.

-Another pint, Marge. If you please.

-Hey, you're drinking fast!

-Hot day, Marge. Feet blistered throat parched. Man needs the sustenance. Also must celebrate. End of a tiring week, after all.

-Oh, boy, what a cute one!

Money on the counter and she casually helps herself. A trustworthy woman. If too obviously promiscuous. After experience nothing but practice. And she's had both. Which my own experience tells me. Whilst enabling me to read those saucy glances she gives me. Not without meaning and rarely ignored. Since I might sample that some sweet night. When the pub doors are shut and the downstairs lights are out. When the beer has been turned off and the Postie turned on. This being a comforting thought. Should the sweet widow Hartnett suddenly decide to turn sour. Which must inevitably happen. Such being love.

Strange to be this far on. And still wanted. Could hardly be the appearance. So put it down to manner of speech. Aided and abetted by my enormous dictionary. Which has made me a gifted talker. Always polite with patience and pride most prominent. Twenty-six years delivering Lizzie's mail and that's what I've finally gained from it. Patience and pride. Both impossible to miss. But with that little bit of steel hidden underneath.

-Hey, Marge, this effin beer's flat!

-It isn't. Just ask Postie here. *He* seems to be enjoying it.

-That I am, Marge. A very nice drop. And so is the barmaid, if I may say so.

-Jesus, if I was younger I'd be blushing. You really *are* a sweetie. Some day, when time permits, I might go for you.

32

You're so romantic, you old goat.

-Watch it, Marge. He's after you. And you know what these postmen are like. Filthy-minded and hot. Even worse than milkmen.

She turns up her nose. At him. While smiling at me. Brassily come-hither as she works the pump-handle. Sounds of splashing beer and clinking glasses and the TV. Here's to Arsenal versus Newcastle, playing you know where, and to Spy Net racing at Sandown. Some horse. I hope. Having placed a small fortune on the four-legged wonder. And if it loses the missus will find out. All hell to pay then. Nasty words and rotten meals for a week. With brain-draining monologues on rent arrears and hire-purchase payments not met. Not to mention the new coat that one had promised to buy her. Without conviction many moons ago. Still. No matter. When you really think about it. Promises, I promise, are made to be broken. And after all, friends. Generosity leads to greed which makes women lust for power. And this married man is having none of that. Give in once, don't you know, and personal freedom is gone for all time. Not that one's a chauvinist. Quite the opposite, in fact. One is all for equality, but a man should be the boss in his own home. Lest anarchy rule.

-Turn that TV off!

-Turn on the radio! They've got the dogs on the radio!

That's it, comrades. Listen for the race results. While looking at the defeated faces turned toward the radio. One of the wonders of modern science. Which in helping us destroys us. Just like television. Where it all starts and ends. For these hopeful aristocrats in their working-class rags. Namely overalls, denims, leather jackets and industrial boots. Eyes squinting through the smoke-haze at that disembodied voice. Enough to terrify a man born a hundred years ago but now commonplace to the lot of us. So off with the visuals and on with the purely oral. Off with the politics and on with the greyhounds. Which are surely more important to the general good. Because they fill and empty pockets. A philosophical thought if ever I heard one.

-Another sausage, please, Marge. With the sauce, of course.

-What *kind* of sauce, Mister Postman?

-Oh, you're so sharp, my sweet. No doubt about that, my love. But it's not *your* kind of sauce I'm after. Too quick with the tongue. Too bold with the eyes. And a man my age too timid to take it. Which is one of life's sad truths.

-Here you are. With sauce. And another pint?

-Blessed are they that understand.

-That's sheer poetry, Postie.

Take a bite, Postie. Full of flavour and scalds the palate. Truly a most marvellous piece of meat. Like other meat we could mention. Deep in the mouth squirting juice onto the tonsils. Cunnilingus being the word employed by those in the know. To describe the actual lip-smacking. Which I try to avoid doing. Content simply to chew and swallow and cool the parched throat. With this excellent pint of bitter. These items combined making an every-day snack. Your average pub lunch. Which uplifts and sustains when the energy falters. And always tastes good. Particularly with the sauce which I truly appreciate. Having heard somewhere that it's good for the eyes. Thus possibly explaining why I've never needed specs. And if good for the eyes then might be good for other things. Recommendations from the lips of the appealing widow Hartnett who doesn't mind the odd beer herself. Nor the small bet now and then. Thereby compensating for the wife. My dearly beloved taskmaster.

Sauce on the lower lip. Flick it away with the index finger. May be a common postman but not without the etiquette. Being one of the finer examples of the ignorant working classes. Yes, that's me. Now casting a lewd eye over Marge's luscious arse. Her skirt tight against it as she bends over for more mugs. The shadow-line of panties. The hint of forbidden holes. And imagine now creeping stark-naked toward her. Member raised and out-thrust and winking suggestively. A creamy tear of joy in its single narrow eye. Then in up to the hilt crying gung-ho and Tarzan. While the onlookers choke on their drinks and sundry delicious snacks.

Such thoughts flash like neon through the mind's dimming light. Forcing one to wonder what the children would say. If they knew. Though probably guessed already. There being no flies upon them. Since this day and age they learn more than mathematics. At school. And once out of it practice what was preached in biology-class. With the little girls frequently much worse than the boys. As exemplified by my own daughter. That cheeky bitch Barbara. Given the way she behaves with that lout, Briggs, another unclean delinquent.

Unclean and unpleasant. Long of hair short of brains. Drinks like a fish, doubtless smokes when out of sight, and probably jumps like a rabbit. Can't say I blame him, though. What with his mother being what she is. Certainly no whore. But no angel either. Once let me have a quickie in return for some drinks out in the back yard of the King's Arms. Standing, too. Most undignified. While the missus was inside knocking back her gin and tonic. Which made it an awful chance to take. Which in turn made it all the more exciting. Human motivation being infinitely complex. Or so Clement Freud said. And so another white-frothing warm beer to calm these feverish thoughts.

-Another pint, please. If you would be so kind. With a sausage and sauce on the side. And my most sincere gratitude.

-Ha, ha, you're becoming bold, Postie. I see the signs.

-Bold, Marge, but not fresh.

-I'll give you that, Postie. You're a gentleman, obviously. I bet you have a nice home and loving wife.

-Alas, unmarried.

-Never?

-Dear wife dead, lo these many years.

-Gee, Postie, I'm really sorry. No wonder you're so quiet.

A little white lie. Not nice but possibly necessary. Never know, after all, when one might require a bit of comfort from that direction. And such statements avoid complications. Such as feminine blackmail. Other means of intimidation when the grapes of love rot. One clearly has her interested. As one is as well. Not being devoid of hope or the willingness to play. And once in there, another warm bed. As well as a few free beers. Not to mention that hot sausage after hours. Served with sauce, of course.

Yummee, yummee. The greyhound races interrupted while electronic voices babble about cigarettes and sundry beverages. Items of which I do not approve. Particularly the cigarettes. Which lead to bad breath and cancer. Of that one can be sure. As someone switches channels to find another sport. The prancing gee-gees. On which bets are won and lost. And one appears to have won. Because here's Mister Murphy. Slapping the shoulder and saying be Jasus ya rogue. In a second will be asked for a beer and what can one do? Civility costs nothing but the price of a drink or two. With no repayment forthcoming. For such are the clichéd Irish immigrants.

And I should know. Father having been one of them. Before the Grim Reaper cut down that fine figure of a man. Who was fond of the women. And anything else that moved. Which alas was his downfall. Twice married and with lots on the side on his labourer's wages. And like father like son. Or so the missus says. When enraged and trying to hurt my feelings. This thought making me remember that I should have been home. Ten minutes ago. Though here I am still drinking. And buying one for Mister Murphy. Who when not in a sober condition is always visibly drunk.

-Well, be Jasus, you've done it again, Postie. First place in the race, ya jammy bastard. And here's you still sittin' here drinkin', ya pig, instead of runnin' down to collect your winnin's. Thanks for the pint. Sure you're a gentleman for buyin' it. A dyin' breed, so I'm told. Not too many left at all. But backbone of the country, salt of the Earth. Remind me to buy ya one in return the next time I'm employed.

A clichéd Catholic clown. But surprisingly shrewd. Could talk the devil into heaven. And would if he wasn't so lazy. Works on an emotional basis. When he feels like it. Or when the rent-man threatens to throw him out of his house. Nevertheless, he survives. Rarely known to buy a drink and never had a complaint. A fact that can only be explained by his size. An ever-smiling psychopathic bone-crusher. Prone to ultra-violent forms of self-expression. Thus ensuring that he frequently spends his nights behind bars. Screaming drunkenly where's the bloody ball and chain. Usually to be released the following morning. An unrepentant jailbird.

-Sure it's a helluva life wit'out a wife but a helluva lot worse if you've got one. Would ya be believin' that foine and beautiful statement, Mister Postman?

-Implicit faith, Mister Murphy, in the enduring goodness of the marital bonds.

-But not married yourself, eh? Not since the passin' away of that sweet woman ya once wedded and bedded in bliss. Not married again since then, eh?

The bastard Irish Mick. Mocking me. Having approached just in time to overhear the conversation between myself and the big-bosomed Marge. Who presently slaves away. As if not hearing a word. But ears flapping to pick up all the gossip. Though learning nothing in this instance. Since a lying tongue and evil mind have I. With an honest countenance. Bland. Enough to melt the heart and loins of most women hereabouts. If not about to fool the grinning Murphy. Who winks lecherously and gives me the thumbs-up. Under the counter to cement our conspiracy. Which greatly amuses him. More so when another pint is placed before him. And me. Though I cannot remember placing the order.

-My thanks, Marge.

-Not at all, Postie.

-God bless.

Slight heat in one's cheeks. Feeling pleasantly embalmed.

While seeing the missus in the cinema of the mind. Drumming her fat fingers. On the kitchen table squinting maliciously. Murmuring homicidal threats with a mouth full of false teeth. Planning to give it to me when I walk through the front door. When she'll compel me to smile in a shamefully humble manner. Offering uneasy jokes and bland cajolery. While secret planning my own brand of vengeance. Knowing the day is coming. When one of us must break. Almost certainly me. Down in the basement sticking pins in a clay doll. A likeness of her. Madly practising my hopefully murderous voodoo. Even recalling that we once met in passion.

-Mister Murphy, I beg of you. Have the second drink on me. When you drink you don't talk which is excellent. So polish that one off.

-Sure you're a real life-saver, Postie. Even if only when blackmailed. Here's to you, however.

-And one for yourself, Marge? For your very kind attention. For no other reason, I assure you.

Smile. Innocently. While being suggestive with twinkling eyes. And observing her mute response. Clearly hinting at possibilities. Which one must bear in mind. The next time the widow Hartnett calls me a black-hearted bastard. As she is inclined to do. Upon occasion. When I spew on the floor and sing sad songs in dulcet tones. Before being ordered to clean up the mess. Using my own handkerchief. Something that Pete Whelan is likely to appreciate. Since vomit is less threatening than blood.

Can't stand the stuff, myself. Blood, that is. Makes me think disturbingly about pain and death. So I give it away. Every six months at the mobile blood bank. For a cup of tea and biscuit. And future insurance. One never knows, after all, when one might need it back. Violence rampant in the streets. All those adolescent hooligans. Kicking sweet old ladies and mild-manner postmen. This being a blot on the city's more civilised aspirations. And widely publicised by the juicier Sunday rags. So must go soon to the blood bank and make another deposit. Might have to make a withdrawal some dark day in the future. When I'm found in the gutter with teeth rattling like castanets. Compliments of some big-booted berk.

Man must plan ahead. For all eventualities. Such as purchasing that pornography for Hans Wernher's mailbox. From foxy Les Wilson. Who leans groggily across the pinball machine. In yonder gloomy corner. So a murmured excuse me. To the hard-drinking Murphy. Then move forward bland-faced through this smoke-wreathed crowd of boozers. With their ricocheting chatter. To the side of the perverted and always shifty Wilson. To lean against the wall beside him. In a pointedly casual manner. And. Not being used to such purchases would burn with shame if caught. For a delicate soul am I. With indelicate intentions. As Wilson glances at me, leering knowingly.

-Feelthy postcards, six for a quid, going, going –

-Gone.

-What? What?

Straightens his spine in response to this rare occasion. His face expressing disbelief. One loud outcry of joy and I'm done for. Man in my position. Caught in sordid transactions. Leading to embarrassing repercussions. So swivel the eyeballs. As cool as James Bond. Silently warning him to keep his trap shut. With tight lips that threaten crude violence for disobedience. As his crooked grin displays rotting teeth. And leprous gums. A meth's drinker from way back. Something I understand. Having once indulged myself. During the first weeks of marriage. When the reality of it struck and turned the world blue. Though one has adjusted since. To marriage and the need for drink. Which does not make me a good man but simply less bad. One who hands over a precious pound note. For six pornographic postcards all the way from Singapore. Genuine Boogie Street material, no less.

How exotic the Far East must be. With its innocent depravity. Must go there some sweet day. Before old age sets in.

The papaya trees, the cheongsams, the honeyed loins. Try some wicked Oriental manoeuvres. Playing with the organ until the sampans come in. But for the moment must content myself. With a journey back to the bar. Hip pocket now bulging with the X-certificate material. While one hand reaches into another pocket for more money. For more beers for myself and the psychopathic Mick, Murphy. Who being of considerable girth can protect me in times of strife. Particularly during brawls that he starts.

Two more pints and damn the groceries. Can Man live by bread alone? Alas, some women seem to think so, including the missus. To whom, it must be said, I don't take too much notice. So down the drink with dignity. Not letting the beer talk. Though this afternoon will tolerate no nonsense from the bitch. Since here I am serving the Queen and her loyal subjects. Which gives me the right to something. Such as these two final beers with an old friend and ally. So order them. And bugger the consequences.

-A foine day to be alive.

-An agreeable statement.

-Sun shinin' in the skies. And young virgins half-naked in the sunshine out there in the pagan streets.

-A sad loss. No doubt. To mankind.

-Skirts swirlin' in the breeze. T'ighs teasin'.

-Quite so.

-And you bein' a postman you'd know.

-What?

-About such t'ings.

-What things?

-Skirts swirlin'. T'ighs teasin'. Cunts callin'. Frustrated housewives and mini-skirted daughters. Longin' for it. Beggin' for it. Principle source of relief to be found in butchers, bakers, milkmen and postmen. Do I speak the truth or not?

-Ask the butchers, bakers and milkmen.

-Ask the butcher indeed. Who hides it in mincemeat and passes it over as mutton. Ask the baker indeed. Who puts it between bread and gives it out as a sandwich. May the saints have mercy, but sure life is a dirty black business. And you'd be seein' it, bein' a postman an' all.

-The postman, like the doctor, is a man of discretion. See all, hear all, repeat nothing. Thus rests this case.

-Save it for Confession, you two-faced git.

This homely pub filling up. Heads bobbing in blue-smoke streams. Blonde Marge working away there like a Trojan. Impressive breasts bouncing. Generous thighs jittery. While fists hammer on the counter and argumentative voices clash. Tingaling, tingaling. The pinball machine. Men on tiptoe throwing darts framed by window-light or TV. Toilet doors opening and closing. With heartening regularity. Reminding this postman of the sudden desperate urge for a piss.

We're in here before we know it. Standing at the trough chiselled out of the concrete floor. Badly stained by the acid of urine and vomit. Man the creator. Of his own liquid waste. Now standing legs apart and unbuttoning his fly. Whistling at the ceiling for the necessary distraction. Then pulling out the sturdy member. Presently shrunken and forlorn. But capable of extension to a length of six-and-a-quarter. Inches. Rigid and blood-engorged. According to an interesting article in a sex-education magazine. Packed with fine thoughts. Not forgetting the photographs. Of unvarnished tit and twat. Stark-naked athletic types in excruciating positions. Highly educational indeed. Especially with the old friend held firmly in the hand. More rigid then than it is at the moment. As with a comforting hiss holy water hits the wall. And splashes onto the boots. To make one a little lighter than one was a second ago. And enabling one to let it drip-dry like an old sock. Then tuck it back in and button up its sleeping bag and walk out again.

-What were ya doin'? Pullin' it off in there?

-Crude, Mister Murphy. Uncultured.

-T'at's me in a nutshell.

Sudden sad yearning for another sausage with sauce. But

decide that self-indulgence has its limits. Instead look for distraction. By looking around the pub. To see a few familiar faces. Fellow postmen and even lower types. Commie cunts to Missus Whittaker. Whose husband sells sweets to little girls and is therefore worth watching. Since we know all about them. The ones who sell sweets to the innocent. And sometimes give the sweets for free in return for you know what. Not that I criticise. Being truly soft of heart. And forgiving of the perversions of others. As I slurp my final pint. Time passing in a dream. Thinking of how reassuring it is to see the faces of enemies. And those one hopes are friends. And to come out slightly ahead. With regard to the friends. Which in these days of trial and tribulation is quite an achievement.

-Would ya be goin' then, Postie?

-The time has come, the Walrus said...

To speak of good Samaritans. Including myself. Worried about the missus. Whose housekeeping money I am spending. About the children. Whom I do not understand. And also concerned for the welfare of ageing spinsters who receive mysterious goods through the mail. From Person or Persons Unknown. Encouraging one to think. That some day I must enter. Eleanor Rigby's house. To search for evidence of the identity of her unknown benefactor. A temptation I have so far avoided and I think I am drunk.

-Am I?

-What?

-Drunk again?

-Yesh.

-Then good day to you.

One last glance at twin mounds. Quivering under wool stretched too tight. And do not let that lewd feminine wink go unnoticed. Instead smile with good teeth flashing. Hopeful as always for tomorrow. And then back through the front door and into this busy thoroughfare. Swaying dangerously in daylight. Passers-by staring at me with barely suppressed disgust. Before pretending they cannot see. Which is why we can ignore them. And straighten the shoulders. Holding high the proud profile and marching onward with dignity. Well aware that the forthcoming afternoon will not be fun. But that tonight. Deep rivers of flesh and the silence of sin.

Homeward bound.

The weary postman.

Chapter Three

-Drunk again.

Glaring at me with bright accusing eyes. The mother of my undisciplined children. Now unattractively plump where once she had been slim. Now contemptuous when once she had been adoring. Such being life. Which a man cannot beat. Yet the injustice of it curdles the blood. While one thoughtfully studies her. The hair-curlers on her head. The smears of cream still on her face. A ripe vision of pulchritude gone to seed. How true it has to be that an ageing crone lies in waiting behind the sweet maidenhead. So remove the peaked cap, straighten the uniformed shoulders, and look the bitch right in the eye. Calmly deny all.

-I *beg* your pardon, dearest?

-You're drunk again.

-*Drunk*, dearest. Did you say... *drunk*?

-You heard what I said.

-I fail to comprehend, desert-flower.

-Don't come none of that malarky with me.

-Your tone of voice, dear, is most unbecoming.

-So's your appearance.

-My *appearance*, lamb?

-Yes, your appearance. Red-eyed and bedraggled.

-I am, as always, the most impeccable postman north of the river.

-Also the most drunken.

-Lies. Flagrant distortions of the truth. Crude exaggerations. I merely stopped off at the King's Arms for a few soothing medicinals. The calories, you know. Good for the stamina. Doctor knows best.

-Always the same. Every Saturday afternoon. Down there guzzling with those drunkards you call friends. And betting, no doubt. Throwing the grocery money away on nags and dogs that never come first. How much was it this time?

-Just a few pence, my dearest.

-How much?

-No more than a few shillings.

-How *much*?

-Five pounds.

-A fiver!

And away she goes. Arms waving histrionically. Face contorted melodramatically. Tongue curling around the area's low colloquialisms. Shouts, shrieks, and a long stream of words not fit for decent Christian ears. Calling upon the mercy of God and various saints. Plus Jesus and Christ and excremental obscenities. Her cheeks colouring like beetroots. The excess fat quivering. An awful sight. Absolutely. And one that makes Ross, our teenage son, remove his gaze from the maze of electric wiring on the carpet. Before, flushing hotly, returning his attention to work on the malfunctioning TV set. A genius forthcoming. Or so we hope.

-A fiver! Oh, God, what have you done? Nothing in the refrigerator but a few cans of beer and a tray of melting ice-cubes. Rent not paid for the past three weeks and the TV licence overdue. Christ in heaven, but what kind of thoughtless monster did I marry? And why? *Why?* When I had so many other offers at the time?

-Scone in the oven, as I recall.

-What a rotten thing to say. And in front of the child himself. You've no feelings. No sense of discretion. Cruel tongue and hard heart. And a filthy liar into the bargain. Lucky for me the boy knows that.

-The boy knows the truth. Which is more than you're

willing to admit.

-Hey, hold on there! Don't drag *me* into your argument!

Glance down to where he kneels on the floor. Offer a winning smile. Shamelessly calculated, but no point in giving opportunities to the opposition. Get the kids on your side of the fence and things might work out for the best. Present and future. One will, after all, require support from those young enough to work. When retirement day comes. Which eventually it must. Besides, he's my son. And that must count for something. Though of what I'm not too sure. Even if he's six-foot tall. And rather awkward on his feet. But with a brain as quick as the electricity with which he likes to dabble. Some day might make good money so for now treat him well. Smiling down at him once more. Before turning back to the missus. All being fair in love and war. And it being her turn.

-There you are, you brute. See what you've just done? You've embarrassed the poor lad. You've *humiliated* him. All that talk about scones in the oven. No wonder the poor thing has a complex.

-I'm not a poor thing, Mum. And I don't have a complex.

-Yes, you have. And don't argue with me. Fine thing when a woman's very own flesh and blood takes sides against her. Such ingratitude! Don't think I haven't been watching you, 'cause I have. You're going the same way as your father, mark my words. Sure you'll end up in jail or in the gutter –

-I've been in neither.

-just like he will if you give him half the chance.

Offensive bitch. Should step right up to her to reaffirm the dignity. And loosen a few of her unpolished dentures. With the back of my not-quite-royal hand. Am only prevented from doing so by gentlemanly instincts. Plus the absolute conviction that she can hit harder. Not worth the pride involved. Especially considering that *my* teeth are genuine. A legacy from more youthful days. Of which she has always been jealous. Particularly because of that night so many nights ago. When she called me a delicious dish. Between her groans of rapture. Then shamelessly begged me to do it to her again. Only to weep afterwards. And call me a seducer of innocence. The hypocrite. Being far from innocent when I first took her. But in fact a trainee nurse who actually asked to inspect it. Before sampling. And once seen not rejected. Simply couldn't help herself. Was at me before I could run away. And in less than an hour almost ruined me for life. Draining good seed with a greed that I was later to pay for. Not the first and certainly not my last passionate moment. Though after that something died a little. Never to be fully regained. And now. Never having been romantic by nature. I fail to comprehend the loss.

Yet loss there has been. So this forthcoming Monday morning. In my personal street of dreams. Will stop to have further words with Miss Lovelorn. Because behind the smile of that girl the secret might lurk. Just waiting to spring forth and tickle my fancy. Though for now return my wandering attention. To the warden of my unholy, imprisoned days. The great bitch-wife, no less.

-A little lunch, dear-heart? Let bygones be bygones and offer a morsel to appease the hunger of this weary man. Such sustenance is needed for the forthcoming week's work. And hard work, beloved, tramping those mean streets. With the heavy mailbag on the shoulder. Work not fit for a man with fine ideals. Your understanding would be appreciated. Also, your cooking.

-No cash, no hash.

-Come, come, all cannot be lost. Not good, you know, to starve one's giver-of-life to the point of malnutrition. Makes for early graves and young widows. Better the loss of five Tory pounds than the loss of really good labour.

-Hmph!

-A pun. Come. I beg you.

-Did you at least *win* something?

-Alas, no.

-Oh, God!

-He looks after your salvation. And mine.

-Hmph!

Rarely fails to work. Temporarily at least. A few sweet words offered with a soothing tone of voice. I know. Having practised it for years. And many have dropped the frilly panties for less. Since it's not what you do but how you word the prelude. And now it's working again. As one sees as clear as day. With the softening of that hard face. And the hint of a smile. Asking once more if I won anything at all. On the gee-gees flogged to death down at Sandown. Smiling even more. When I say that I didn't bet. And proving it by handing over a full wage packet. Without mentioning the packet that I won. Some secrets being best kept. Particularly since the knowledge of the winnings not yet collected. Is more than a modest comfort. Since it can be spent grandly. Tonight unbeknownst. To the wife and offspring. Because a man in these hard times must look after himself. And one has to be cruel. To be kind.

-A full wage! I can't believe my own eyes!

-Integrity is all.

-It'll cover the back rent. But no groceries.

-I can see in yonder cupboard the last of the sausages. And can almost taste them on the tongue. Believe me, dear-heart, the appreciation would be boundless. And fear not for the forthcoming week. For one is still not without the influence. And after your good cooking I shall feel strong enough to make my way to Joe Greenwood's corner-shop. Still good for the helpful credit there. Joe tends to be suspicious but is not without heart in the face of a tragic story well told. You have my word that further rations with be forthcoming. Now the sausages. Please. If you will.

Retreats back into her kitchen. Mumbling and moaning. But another round won. By me, of course. Which makes me flush with pleasure. While removing the peaked cap, the jacket and boots. To sit down in this deep chair. And contemplate upholstery jobs that will never be done. Broken springs in torn fibre. For character, not comfort. Wiggling the toes in the holy socks. Also unwashed. Thus smelling like something the cat dragged in. Though we haven't a cat.

Note that the son, still squatting on the floor, is twitching his nose at my curling toes. Pretend not to notice. Whilst feeling perfectly comfortable. With the lack of a bath or shower. Have heard others claim that this is the Affluent Age. But don't think I'm a member of the club. Though feel contented. In my modest, bitter way. Wanting to watch the TV. But can't because young Ross has the tube out. And is fiercely studying that complex of many-coloured wires. Encouraging me no end. Thinking of him going far. And taking me with him. I hope. Gratitude being in order. Since though he may have been an accident he has not been ignored. The hint of kindness still alive in this heart turning cold. Also understanding. Which showed when occasionally I let him do as he wished. Beg, borrow or steal. A generosity of spirit that possibly kept us from loathing one another. So right now a few intimate words would not go amiss.

-Tell me, son. What do you do?

-I'm studying the workings of this bloody thing.

-The word *thing* is sufficient. There is no blood on it.

-I want to learn how it works.

-You're interested in electronics?

-Greatest thing since sliced bread.

-Good that you should think so. I myself have always been a believer in progress. Infinite faith in the potential of television, space-flight, rock music and revolution. Man must move forward. Even unto oblivion. It is the duty of we elders to keep up with the changing times. Shrink the trousers and broaden the outlook. My next pair of boots, if ever I can afford them, shall be made of Marrakech leather. You can be certain of that.

-Christ, Dad, you talk funny.

-Strange.

-All right, then, strange.

-Language requires precision, son. Just like the electrics you so enjoy tinkering with. Always bear this truth in mind. Just because you're the son of a common postman doesn't mean you should talk like a common navvy.

-Ah, hell, Dad, give it a go. It's just that you've a talent with words. You should have been on radio.

-Quite true, son. Your point is acknowledged. Each to his own, I suppose. And with skill such as yours, you should go far. Rather see you working at electronics than humping bags filled with letters and parcels. If you could comprehend the indignity of my position, you would surely weep.

-You're not doing too bad, Dad.

-If clues were shoes I'd be barefoot.

Thus ends the Sermon on the Mount. For talk is time wasted. Or so says this sage. As he listens to sizzling sausages. And sniffs their heady aroma. Which is fit for a king and helps me to feel that I am one. Leaning back in this armchair. And conjuring up perverse visions. Of long-legged ladies writhing nude in spaghetti. Or dancing lewdly on antique tables piled high with pig-shit. This doubtless being symbolic. But of what I do not know. So perhaps should be interviewed. By some loony psychologist. Or psychiatrist. And watch him disintegrate while trying to pick his teeth. And this elusive brain. Since if genius and madness are truly twins, then genius I surely am. And like father. Like son.

-Fucking tube. These shitty connections.

Wish I could talk more to the boy. But the interest never lasts long. Hardly more than five minutes. Which is sad since he *is* a pleasant lad. Thankfully devoid of hooligan tendencies. And hasn't yet come in saying I need to get married. Stuck it in her and now she's up the spout. So sometimes I love him. In my fashion. Whilst upon other occasions am possessed of the urge to hurl him through the shuttered front windows. Tape-recorder, record-player, blue denims and all. Having only refrained out of respect for civility. Plus the knowledge that old age will force me to lean upon him. Life being indifferent to the old and infirm.

Neither of which I am yet. Though my time will surely come. As the wife is now coming. With the sausages.

-A treat, dear. And done as only you can do them. Yummee, yummee. Delicious. Indeed, the only word is *exquisite*. A fine day it was, dear, when you and I were wed. The simple home life. Good family, decent food. What more, may I ask, could one want?

-Rent money.

-Please, dear, not while I'm eating. Causes the indigestion and sleepless nights. And these sausages are done so superbly. Very nice, the feel of this hot plate on my lap. Makes me recall many pleasant memories. Of you and I. And youth's passion. And so on and so forth.

-God, the things you say in front of the child!

-I'm not a child, Mum!

-True. The child is no longer a child. And shame should not be part of his make-up. If he doesn't learn from us he'll only learn from the alley-cats. And we'll have no frustrations in this house.

Munch on these sausages and observe the lad blushing. Nice to see youth with all its tormenting secrets. But strange that the boy should be so shy and his sister so bold. Have never been prejudiced against bastards. But others don't think the same way. So perhaps he was victimised at school. And didn't tell anyone. How heroic that would make him if it were true. One modest hero in this house.

The girl is legitimate. And already no spring chicken. Have noticed that lewd look in her eyes. And the way she sneaks in during the early hours of the morning. Hair dishevelled hemline up to her navel. Possibly covered in lice from the unwashed torso of that lout Briggs. Whose mother I once had in an undignified manner. In the open air not breathing fresh air. So possibly the resentful creature later informed her son. And he in turn looks to my daughter for vengeance. As well as his selfish pleasure. Making unchaste my once chaste dearly beloved. Who in doing it would certainly not be doing it for the first time.

Yet perhaps one is wrong. Though one looks for the signs. Of the ominous swelling of the svelte teenage belly. No indications at the moment. But if that should ever happen her mother would kill her. Though not I. Since the memory of adolescence has not left this ageing mind. Nor cast out the understanding that helps one to accept. That young blood runs hot and nature takes its course. As it surely must. Frustration leads to insanity and we want none of that in this house. Prefer to let the young frolic. Exhaustion comes soon enough. And, since this excellent meal is finished, the missus may finish as well. The washing-up.

-I am finished. The plate. Please remove it.

-Haven't you got no legs?

-Not *no*. Any.

-Any what?

-Legs.

-Whose legs?

-Your legs.

-What about them?

-Get them moving. Back to the kitchen. And take this plate with you when you go.

Grabs the plate and departs. Not thinking. Since she rarely does. Being possessed of a brain like a scrambled egg. Which is a handy thing to have in a wife. Now back in her place in the kitchen. Doing the washing-up. While I watch the TV set reassembled by my son. Screen flickering back to life. And filled with football players. A worthy game. Bringing out the beast in man. Really rather sexual. And there is my boy. Still squatting on the floor. Reading an electronic's magazine. A good lad. Soon to support me. If he did but know it.

-Yeah, yeah, doodeedah!

Here comes the daughter. Smartly down the stairs. In gleaming white hipster-jeans and a skimpy halter. Belly-button exposed and the rest of her shapely. Singing yeah, yeah and doo-dah. While she shakes the long legs. And applies phosphorescent lipstick to lush, knowing lips. To be seen this evening in a trance of abandonment. Gyrating those hips in a lewd, enticing manner. Long hair whipping around her face. While she pouts voluptuously. In order to tease young Briggs. Into a hot lather. Which will later be cooled. In the rear-seat of his car with its fall-back upholstery. The greatest incentive to free love being the modern automobile. Warm and roomy with a radio and barber-shop contraceptives. In what was once only the glove compartment. And now my daughter, risking pneumonia, again shakes her naked hips.

-Yeah, yeah! Doodeedah!

Knuckles knocking on the front door announcing the arrival. Of slimy lover-boy Briggs. A tall streak in suede jacket and tight, revealing trousers. Reminding me of that French bird. Brigitte Bardot. Because of his long hair. And feminine, pouting lips. Which means I fail to comprehend. Such transvestite traits in the modern adolescent male. But say nothing in order to prove that I am one of the In Set. And that surely is me. A corrupt, swinging daddy of the Space Age. A heel glued to the inset.

-Hi, mate!

-I am not your mate, Mister Briggs. I am your girlfriend's father.

-Sorry, sir.

Will not tolerate such impudence from the young. Familiarity breeds contempt and I won't have a bar of it. Bad enough to think that I'll likely get him for a son-in-law. An awesome possibility. From which this family might never recover. The whole illustrious line. Of working-class heroes. Shot to hell because of one lousy addition.

It's not the sex I mind. I have an open mind, after all. But I do believe he's encouraging her to smoke and drink. Indeed, I must ask her about it. Some fine day. When I have both the courage and the energy. But for the moment will content myself. With thoughts of my own approaching evening. And the widow

Hartnett's welcoming embrace and all it will lead to.

-Gee, Dad, you're way out in that fantastic jacket. I mean, it just knocks me dead, man!

-Pardon?

-Oh, not *you*, Dad. Dad's just a *phrase*, silly. I mean Briggs, here.

-Ah, I see.

My weekly conversation with the daughter has just ended. A delicate task performed well. So she takes Briggs' grubby hand and off they both go. Out through the front door and into his battered car. Then away with a belching of poisonous fumes.

A remarkable turn of events. When the children can afford more than their parents. But such are the ways of this wicked old world. Lots of good men died on the battlefields of Europe for this. Not one of them myself but served well on the home front. Having wriggled out of conscription by becoming a postman. It was not that I feared death. But merely that I loved life. Which gave me certain inalienable rights. As well as the firm belief. That it is better to live for one's country than to die for it. Also helps the taxman. Something that the dependents of dead heroes have failed to understand. And. Come to think of it. A blight on democracy that I never received a medal. Only sore feet, a chafed right shoulder and a great deal of weariness.

-Suppose you're going out tonight, then?

-As usual, dear wifey. The lads will be expecting me about seven.

-More drinking.

-Darts.

-Hmph. When will you be back?

-Difficult to say, beloved. You know what the lads are like. Might be forced to drink more than I can take and have to spend the night with Mister Murphy.

-Hmph. That one. Just like all the Irish. Hasn't washed for six months and sleeps in his Wellington boots. Why don't you try to find some *decent* company for a change? You might have become an inspector years ago if you'd mixed with a better class of person. Like your superiors at work, for instance. No wonder you're still pounding the bloody pavements.

-Just pavements, dear. There is no blood on them. And I *enjoy* pounding the pavements. Makes for the occasional interesting encounter. Enables one to see more of life. Stimulates the mind and discourages boredom. How many can work out in God's clean air?

-Hmph.

An eloquent woman. Who despises me for being what I am. Like most common women is obsessed with class. Even admiring the Royal Family. And when asked by friends what her husband does for a living she blushes and lowers her head in shame. Thus causing me to despise *her* in turn. Thus ensuring that the circle is complete.

Sometimes feel that marriage is a form of mutual cannibalism. Each partner rending the flesh of the other. But. If this is true. She will not see these old bones exposed. Since against Socratic calm she has no weapon. Except the withholding. Of the matrimonial rights. Something at which she is well practised.

Yet I benevolently ignore this distasteful tactic. Not being a savage when it comes to human frailty. Forgive-and-forget being the maxim of the true gentleman. Thus the bad feelings between us don't come from this tender heart. Meaning that death will carry me to the gates of the righteous. Or would if I still believed. Though alas I do not. As I now rise to prepare to go out for the groceries. And later prepare for the evening frolics. Small comfort to a sad man. Who will wash his face, brush his teeth, pamper his hair and dress in his only suit.

Dark is the evening but bright is the soul.

Eternally young.

Chapter Four

A couple of ales. A few friendly words. A little bit of love and a man has the world at his feet. Which eases the tensions and makes life worth living. Now. Here. In this early-evening hour in the noisy smoky hole of the King's Arms. Surrounded by jostling bodies and straining voices. Offering a lot of movement and a great deal of shouting. While on yonder small stage an amplified pop group is creating ear-splitting sounds. As well as burgeoning headaches. Young hoodlums the lot of them. With lean, acned faces. As drunk as the customers. Perhaps even high on pot. Leering at the young tarts who leer back without shame. And spit chewing-gum on the floor. Of this art-inspiring proletarian pub.

We're the trendy thing, so I'm told. New working-class heroes with hearts of pure gold. Worshipped by the intellectuals of the respectable Sunday papers. And by filthy-rich pop stars. Not that I blame them. As I glance cagily around me. Seeing the stuff of which poetry is made. Life in the raw without false inhibitions. Which is just what the culture-vultures like. To talk about. The hypocritical shits. Who wouldn't actually be seen dead in this place.

Yes, indeedy. Life in the raw. Stoned winos with toothless gums winking at bag ladies. Who'll do it for a pint of bitter or a packet of crisps or a fag. Drunkards, delinquents and decadent dolly-birds. With thighs you could part with a smile. Oh me, oh my, but life *does* go on. Leaving us too old to handle it. Red-eyed as the missus said. Forgetting the pot-belly and ulcers. The hurting feet and aching bones. As those around one shout and sing and swear like troopers and smash glasses. And the barmaids succumb to edgy nerves.

Mister Murphy to my left. Archie Brown to my right. Stout friends. And true. My bodyguards two. Ready with their fists. Should bullies threaten the gentle postman. Or with lies to the missus. Who believes I'll be staying with Mister Murphy tonight. When I'll actually be in the bed of the welcoming widow Hartnett. Performing in an invigorating variety of positions. To calm the fears of September years. And she enjoys it that way, so the satisfaction is mutual. And serves notice that I'm not a male chauvinist.

Sip this ale and smile politely. At the lewd Missus Briggs. As she nods suggestively. Toward the back door. Doubtless recalling knee-tremblers from the not-so-distant past. Shocking sort that she was once. And still is. With that lout of a son. Who seeks to corrupt my once incorruptible daughter. Who is now shrewd and sexy. Making me think it very strange. That I've never felt desire for that particular offspring. That otherwise highly desirable piece. Must be something to do with the hormones. Or subconscious guilt. Man must be careful. Lest the beast break loose. Too hideous to contemplate so quickly have another sip. Of this excellent beverage. And one-thousand blessings. On the soothing amber fluid. Whilst listening to inebriated Archie Brown moving in for the kill.

-First place to Spy Net, Postie, and you backed it. How much did you win?

-A few pence, Mister Brown. No more.

-Lying cunt. You bet a fiver if you bet a bean. At the least.

-Come, come, such extravagance is beyond me. Where, pray, would I obtain such an amount?

-By avoiding the rent-man.

-A scandalous notion.

-You're loaded with loot, you tight-arsed bastard. And my larder is empty. With heartless creditors hammering on the front door. You know I wouldn't ask if I wasn't desperate. But I bleed to death and only you can help me. A fiver from your winnings and I'll see you the next time I get a job.

-If money was honey this bee would be dead. Sorry, but the postman can't help you.

-Jesus Christ, did you hear that, Mister Murphy? Did you lay your earlobes on this heathen's disgraceful lie?

-I heard it. With me own great flappin' ears I heard it. An' a shockin' untruth it was too.

-Gentlemen, you wrong me.

-You can't be wrongin' the very devil himself.

-Please.

-Up me with a Tory prick if I don't speak the truth. But if a man was dying of thirst, this postman wouldn't give him a drink of spit. Postie, what kind of a heartless bastard are you? Make it two quid and we'll call it quits.

-Two pounds to you and my family would starve for a fortnight. Also, I'm saving up to pay the rent-man. Would you turn me into a charlatan, Mister Brown?

-One quid.

-Marge, dearest, three more pints. For myself and my thirsty friends.

Nothing like a free beer. To shut Archie Brown's cadging mouth. A likeable gent but distressingly relentless. When it comes to matters of money. An incorrigible scrounger. Lots of withdrawals but no deposits. Lend to him once and get lumbered for life. Him taking the view that the bank's always accessible. With the customer always taking. Never putting back in. Of course one is all for helping the odd friend in need. But charity begins at home. And should definitely stay there. Not that my family receives too much of it. Since I don't believe in spoiling the troops. Which would only leave them unprepared. For future hardships. And me unprepared. For expensive Saturday nights. With cold beer and warm thighs. Those basic necessities which rarely are free. Since nothing is any more. Nor in fact ever was. Such being life. The dream of existence. Shadows passing shadows in cigarette-smoke haze. In which I sip this fine brew. And contemplate the hours still to come. When love shall briefly shelter me from chaos. As well as from drunkenness.

-Am I?

-What?

-Drunk again.

-Yesh.

-Terrific.

Sense troubles arising. On yonder small stage. Which is vague in the smoke-haze. Beyond a sea of flushed faces. Eyes red-rimmed and enlarged. All desperately desiring to have a good time. As one sits here feeling that hysteria lurks. At the bottom of beer glasses. While the well-laced Jack Collins grabs the microphone on the stage. Rudely out of the hand of the youth who was singing. Obviously seeking to give a free rendition of his own filthy song. About China, Chile and sex. Or China, chilli and sex. With his stained shirt-tails flapping and his dentures askew. Clinging to his lower lip. Which makes for a pretty sight. As he spits four-letter words such as if you see kay. All over the lead guitarist. Who promptly shoves him aside with a rough navvy's hand. Glittering rings on the fingers. For the sharp edge they lend to the tightening knuckles. Particularly in moments of hooligan violence. And behind those guitars. Four hooligans lurk. With gravel in their voices and steel in their hearts. Being the misbegotten seed of frenetic times. Misunderstood under the flashing neon signs. Or so say the pundits in the loftier Sunday rags. Explaining why these teenagers are so quick at lashing out. With yeah-yeahs and bovver-boots. These being interesting philosophical speculations. Evolving out of the teeming thoughts. Which we could discuss on Monday with the sneering Hans Wernher. Before dropping the porn photos into his hallway. To later be perused. While on his celibate's lap. Hopefully leading to a Saint Vitis dance of frustration. Which should be pathological. At the least. If I know my birds and bees.

-Hey, keep this old cunt away from the stage!

One of the musical hoodlums. Pushing Jack Collins away. Forcing him backwards between two tables arse over tit on the floor. Where he scrambles about like a crab. Eyes glazed with humiliation. The blood draining from his face. To the tune of mocking laughter and scattered booing.

-Leave 'im alone, you arrogant young git!

One already fat lady expanding rapidly like a soufflé. Face red with anger and clenched fists raised on high. A man-killer for sure. Bawling abuse at the band. In language not soothing to sensitive ears. While the acned delinquent scowls becoming nervous. And drowns her obscenities with his amplified guitar. Which he holds in a masturbatory pose. Sliding his fingers up and down it. Until the quivering soufflé sits down again, still glaring self-righteously.

Peace. For the moment restored. Ensuring safe entrance to the Salvation Army lady. Who weaves determinedly through this rough crowd. Using guilt to bring in money. Frowning upon drink. Though not upon the booty it raises for her cause. This being in my view a most despicable hypocrisy. To which I refuse financial contribution. Moral outrage being strengthened by my reluctance to part with hard cash. Not easily earned. Which helps one to stare steadily at her penetrating, accusing gaze. And say no. With a smile that smacks of sympathy. And understanding. Until she turns away and moves off through the noisy, smoke-wreathed crowd. While I take in the comments of learned friends.

-What a nerve they have!

-Beggin' money from the poor!

-Up her fat Christian arse!

-With a broomstick.

-And a good bit of this.

-Nothin' like a bit of religion with your bit of relief.

-Now the old Postie, here. He gets plenty of relief without the religion.

-A sad loss, gentlemen. I drift toward death, unblessed.

-An' a worse creature for it.

-Untrue.

-Bein' hard of heart.

-Untrue.

-An' uncarin' when it comes to the needs of others.

-Such as?

-That loan you won't give to Archie, here. Who needs it less than I do. But wit' more conviction.

-My pockets bleed, Postie. My belly rumbles. Eviction and potential starvation loom larger each day.

-Get a job, Mister Brown.

-You're bein' cruel, Postie. When all I need is a little help. From a flush friend who squats on a mountain of greed. Preserving his gelt while losing his soul. The Irishman here knows. As all Irish Micks do.

-To be sure. Least he can do is buy another round.

-Agreed. Waiter! I say, *waiter*!

-Yes, sir. No need to shout, sir.

Finally pausing at our table this unfriendly creature. With a tray in one hand and resentment in his face. Which is pale, pimpled and thoroughly unpleasant. A member of the criminal fraternity, doubtless.

-Waiter, you ignored me.

-I did not.

-Deliberately.

-I did *not*!

-Three more pints. Unspilled. And be quick about it.

-*Yes*, sir!

Away between the other tables. His metal tray glinting golden. Over the bobbing heads. And veils of blue smoke. Under the blazing light-bulbs. And the television set. Which has Lulu looking luscious shrieking singing. Enormous eyes staring down like big spoons on the waiter's retreat.

-Did youse hear that? Did youse hear that wee git? Would ya credit the cheek of him?

-Sure he's just a bit hungry. For a good knuckle-sandwich. And will get one if he isn't too careful.

-Gentlemen. Please. It is Saturday evening. We want simple relaxation, not a rough-house. Forgive and forget is the motto. A little Christian charity goes a long way. Which all of us should know.

-Forgiveness or fear, Postie?

-Charity or cowardice, Postie?

-Gentlemen, you wrong me. I merely have concern for my fellow man and am willing to show it.

A slight dizziness in the head. Vision going out of focus. Usually feel that inebriation is highly undignified, but this evening a mad dog is biting. Great turbulence within. Gradually filling me with the urge. To do something inane. Such as indecent exposure. By vigorously slapping down on that Salvation Army collection-plate something more substantial than mere money. After which. Look directly at her stunned face. And say feed *that* to your starving multitudes. Giving her the thrill of her life. And me a five-year jail sentence. Not worth the titillation in the thought but giving rise to fresh hunger.

Sausages. Must buy some on the way home. To the warm widow Hartnett. Or would if the shops were still open. To unwrap them lovingly in her kitchen upon arrival. And let them be sizzled on her modern electric cooker. To be consumed before devouring female flesh. Since they add to the vigour and enhance the performance. Leading to womanly gratitude in the wee small hours. Of the morning and pearly dawn. Which I prefer not to dwell upon as the harassed waiter returns. To angrily bang our three pints down on the table. Thus splashing the beer about. Thus causing six eyes to turn upwards. All brightened by outrage.

-Did youse see that, lads?

-All over the fuckin' table. And the insolent bastard did it deliberately.

-Execrable manners, gentlemen. And has the impertinence

to look forward to a tip.

-Which he won't get.

-Unless he comes back with fresh glasses. Filled to the brim.

-Naturally.

A sharp blade of excitement here. Which though disgraceful is irresistible. Mister Brown's navvy fingers drumming dramatically on the table. And Mister Murphy's face alight with Gaelic self-righteousness. Causing the waiter to take a step back. Swallowing his prominent Adam's apple in nervousness and anger. Snake-eyes flitting left to right. Taking all of us in as we take *him* in. A mean young man with thick grease in his black hair. Common. Yes, indeed. And now clearing the phlegm from his choked throat. To spit out his belligerence.

-Hey, watch it! We want no trouble here. Just pay for those drinks and no smart comments. Put up and shut up.

Well, deary me, the grossness. To talk to regular customers in such a manner. Service clearly isn't what it used to be. Lacking in civility and the other social graces. Whatever they are. Still, it's unacceptable. One has to admit this. Should rake this particular gentleman fore and aft. With a pair of knuckle-dusters. Before throwing his battered carcass into the gutter outside. Where it certainly belongs. But refrain from doing so. Because he might hit back. Instead decide that a few pertinent words would not be amiss. And that I'm the man to offer them. Speak now. Or forever hold your peace.

-You, my good man, have the shameless ill manners of an orang-utan suffering from diarrhoea. One more word of insolence from that syphilitic tongue and I'll have this wretched pub razed to the ground. Now kindly depart and return with three fresh pints before my friends unhinge your flapping jawbone. Stop bouncing your outsized goolies together and simply do as you're bid.

-Don't you fuckin' talk to *me* like that!

Throws his tray to the floor and takes a step forward. Which is as far as he gets. As this postman leaps up. A pint of beer in his right hand. Free. On the house. A drink not to be missed. While Murphy. The Irishman. With the growl of a gorilla. Dives over the table with both arms outstretched. Hands reaching for the waiter's throat. To grip firmly and squeeze on the bobbing Adam's apple. Forcing the pop-eyed lout back down to the floor.

-Oh, my God!

-Jesus Christ!

Women shrieking men swearing at one another. And two or three other tables crashing over. With much smashing of glass. As Murphy and the waiter roll about on the floor. In the broken glass and spilt beer of the toppling tables of this untidy pub. Which degenerates swiftly into an arena. Where it's each man for himself and to hell with the women. Unfortunately so. As the postman hides away in this cosy safe corner. Gulping his free beer. And observing the glittering grace of shards of glass in flight. At trajectories conducive to aeronautical aesthetics. To land upon the stage. Between amplifiers and tangled cables. Already deserted by the young brutes with broad belts. Having doubtless plunged happily into the bloody fray. To stomp, strike and lash. While the Postie grabs hold of a large glass of whiskey. Off the nearest upright neglected table. And downs it rapidly for the courage to be found in it.

-Fuckin' cunt!

-Rotten shit!

Appalled by such language. Not to mention the violence. Contemplate the fighting on all sides and wince each time a blow lands. Uncivilised for sure. Being devoid of the dignity. And making me glad to be in here instead of out there. Never *was* one for violence. And always refused to encourage it in others. For fear that it might be directed at me with painful results.

-Watch that bastard!

-You bitch!

Beyond flailing fists and colliding bodies the manager is dialling the police. And the violence being intimidating. To say the very least. We must shamelessly on hands and knees make our retreat. Along this shit-brown wall. Under legs gross or shapely which frequently offer. A unique view of the world. As the vanquished groan and fall. Left and right to the floorboards. Making me feel concern for the pearly-white molars. Which could receive the brunt of an accidental boot. Or high-heeled shoe. Thus ruining the appearance. Of this charming personality. Who is now close to the front door. And jumping to his feet. And taking a deep breath for both courage and energy. Before grabbing an almost-full bottle of whiskey. From another neglected table. Guiltily excited while making a run for it. Into the dark and cooling night air. Where peace descends like a white dove.

Along the street at a lively gait. Tucked under the loose coat this bottle of stolen booze. Making an unnatural bulge. Which could make for dark suspicions. Though this a respectable street. No policemen about. Lights indoors glowing behind clean curtains. Warmly beckoning in the darkness. Where young lovers groan ecstatically. In sheltering doorways. Illuminated softly in the dim light of the street-lamps. And high above, a low sky. So tonight it might rain. Upon the rooftops of the houses in which casual lovers lie. Such as myself and the willing widow Hartnett.

Better take care. A gang of long-haired louts laughing raucously at yonder corner. Though hopefully will not bother an old man. Who keeps his peace. And delivers their saucy magazines in plain-brown envelopes. Thus helping their hot tools to vibrate in the hand. Now raising my own. Meaning the hand alone. And offering a friendly nod when I pass leaving laughter behind. As they talk of sexual matters. In terms shocking to the elderly. The young not being at all romantic. In the company of one another. But almost certainly when alone in the privacy of their thoughts. Though we are never to know. What others truly think. Especially when young. As I was so many years ago. When I still had some dreams left.

A long walk this. One that seems to take forever. Yet eventually ends. At the house of the widowed Peggy Hartnett. In this quiet street of dreams unfulfilled. Tucked away. In the darkness. Which shields us at times from discomfiting truths. While one glances left and right. In case enemies should be peeping. At me. For the scandal. Then knock, knock on the door. Listening for keen footsteps. Which are heard soon enough. Treading lightly but quickly. And stop when the brass flap of the mailbox is pushed out. And a voice emerges from it. Whispering who is it? Frightened. As she is. Of nocturnal villains. Raping. Robbing. According to the more sensational Sunday newspapers. Which God help us we all enjoy reading.

-'Tis I, the bogey man.

Said with a chuckle. To relax the nervous creature. Who now opens the door and whispers:

-Quick!

Which I am. Scurrying inside. Brushing against her as I wonder about this brazen duplicity. Which being shameless makes life more exciting. And love more ennobling. So once inside, with the door closed again, he turns to face his dark lady.

-Tell me, my true love. Do you enjoy the odd sausage now and then?

-Don't be rude.

-The kind that one cooks.

-Occasionally.

-Then you would have some in the kitchen?

-Yes.

-Wonderful. Must feed the belly before we treat the loins. Was going to bring some with me. But in my eagerness to get to the King's Arms I let the thought slip from the mind. Would be appreciated if one could hear some sizzling in the frying-pan. With an egg perched on top like a little bird.

-You're drunk.

-A case of slight intoxication. But harmless and of good cheer. Now the sausages, my beauty. If you will.

-What happened to you? There's spilt beer all over you. And pieces of glass stuck to your soaked coat.

-Ran into a double-decker bus. Slightly bruised but otherwise unharmed. The bus, unfortunately, is a mess.

-Deary me, aren't *you* the one? Take that coat off and I'll sort it out later. And I suppose I'd better fetch you those sausages. To help you recover from the shock of that bus.

-You're so kind, my angel.

Off with the coat and shoes. Sink into this modish pink armchair. A strange piece of furniture in tune with the Space Age. All sleek lines and curves. But undeniably comfortable. Only to a dead dog or a man made of rubber. But wiggle the holy toes. Unscrew the cap of this whiskey-bottle. For the warmth it provides. Before the cold sheets of the bed. Though not to be cold for long. Meanwhile a sneaky sip of this healing beverage. My lady slaving away there in the kitchen. Peg O' my heart. Still wearing the austere black dress of the businesswoman that she is. Still attractive. For her age. As all women must want to be. Even when cooking sausages. And producing rich aromas. This particular woman being a fine cook. Amongst her other endowments.

Her husband dead and buried. Once installed gas appliances. But a lazy man. No commonsense. Fell asleep beside a main's tap. With the gas turned on which turned him right off. Permanently. So was quietly cheaply buried. Leaving Peggy free to improve her situation. And pick-and-choose her men. Most of whom were decent chaps without much interest to her. Until I entered the picture. Whispering suggestive words while delivering the Queen's mail. To soon be invited into her large bouncing bed. Gratuities unbeknownst to one's post office superiors. Who might have had a fit. Or started wanting it for themselves. Corruption always descending from the top to ease the working man's guilty conscience.

Such thoughts make me realise. That I could not stay the course. Were it not for such comforting liaisons. So blessed be the womb of woman. From which all goodness doth flow. And blessed be the sausages now resting upon my lap. On the warm plate placed there by the efficient Peggy Hartnett. Phallic and piping hot. To build up the strength I will need for the forthcoming marathon.

-A lovely feed, Peggy. Vital to these old bones.

-Not so old.

-Not so young.

-Where did you get the whiskey?

-Backed a winner, dear-heart. So bought it to celebrate. Thought it might help you survive the long nights without me.

-You've never been that extravagant in your life. Where did you *really* get it?

-An old friend gave it to me. When nostalgically recalling the retreat from Dunkirk. An ordeal we shared together. When you and I were young, Maggie.

-You were never in the war.

-Luckily I had no need to show him my battle-scars. And who really remembers who fought beside whom? Or where? Or when? Could I disillusion a senile old friend who insists that we once fought side by side? I, who believe in fairy tales?

-What an entertaining liar you are.

She smiles. And stands upright preparing for bed. Making me feel young again. Temporarily, at least. As I sip this fine whiskey, knock back these sausages, and dwell on life's mystery and tragedy.

Always difficult preparing to go to bed with a woman. Without recalling the first time. A long, long time ago. When the postman was barely more than a child. A self-conscious adolescent, to be precise. All superficial arrogance and secret despair. Fumbling, groping and drowning in his inadequacy. Later, helpless tears and babbling about love. I love you I want you I need you as he wept. Though knowing in his heart that such love did not exist. Or at least did not endure. For the alley was dark and cold and littered with rubbish. Making us at one.

With the cats howling in heat. Never again to look with honesty at one another. All passion spent in that singular single night. Beyond hope of recovery. Fifteen years old and tormented by lust. And love. Or the dream of a love that would never materialise. Time passing too quickly and other events intervening. Such as careless ejaculations, shotgun wedding, children, the swift flow of disappointing years. Until youth was gone and the bitter lessons learnt. With a shrug. And a smile. In tribute to the myths. Which endlessly beguile and then betray us.

Now, here, at the crossroads of the night. Preparing for the satisfaction of more knowing flesh. Without dreams. Without bitterness. With understanding. And need. And the confidence of small expectations.

-Are you ready?

-I am.

-Then come on.

She stands by the bed. Unfastening her brassiere. A silent, soulful silhouette. This being my one romantic cliché for the night. As I tread across the carpet to enter the bathroom. White tiles clean and shiny. Bright as the mirror into which I now gaze. Studying lines of age in the cold, revealing glass. But smiling. With defiance. Before placing between the fingers this plastic-handled toothbrush. All my very own. To polish the healthy molars. With the peppermint toothpaste. For the annihilation of bad breath. Or so TV has informed me. In my hitherto fore appalling working-class ignorance. Now washed away with water. Hot from a steaming tap. Which is a luxury I cannot afford in my own cold-water home. Due to excruciating overheads. Such as betting and beer. Small comforts in a sad world. The tingling skin to be dried. With this flowered, deluxe towel. Then back to the bedroom where my lady lies in waiting. Not panting. Not demanding. Perfectly quiet and at peace. Wanting it for the sanity. If nothing else.

-You look funny when you're starkers.

-But observe. No belly.

-That's because you're sucking it in.

Ignore the accusation. Slide between these crisp sheets. Feel the cold cloth and warm skin wrapped around you. Breasts. Thighs and belly. Expectant nipples stiffening keenly. A quickening pulse of anticipation in the groin as the heat quickly rises. Mmm. How nice. The female as paradise. As we burrow in more deeply. Blankets up to the chin. And sigh. Almost sadly. But actually in relaxation. And smile. Hiding greed. The hunger that lurks within us all. Particularly in moments such as this, the helpless yearning, the need. Turning to her body. Fingers closing around her tits. Her lips against mine as her fingers slide along it. Making it rise. Not as rigidly as in youth. But enough to do the job. Satisfactorily. Humming. As she holds it while it throbs. Her fingers tickling the balls. Charging them like a battery. Which in turn charges the blood. Electrically flowing to make the flesh ripple. From the head down the spine along the thighs to the stretched legs and curling toes. Giving life to an inner light. While we breathe hard and grope blindly. Exploring curves and hollows, matted mounds and damp grottoes. With impertinent hands. And mounting desire. While lovingly whispering filth. Into her burning ear. Which is chewed almost raw as one slowly sinks down. Between her raised thighs. In order to start moving. In a timeless motion. Of advance and retreat. Thrust and withdrawal. In and out in a trance. Briefly filled with omnipotence. Eternally young. In these green-dark tides of time without pity. No pain. No bitterness. No dread for the future. Just pleasure. Incandescence. The illusion of boundless freedom. Before the spasm hammers home the blind floundering seed. Returning us to Earth. And our sorrows. And the need for a piss.

Chapter Five

He slept.

And went along the dark river between the shimmering green banks toward the black waves, white-flecked, iridescent. The river flowed into twilight through the harsh jungle chatter, under huge beating palms with their silvery dew. Now night, now day, now full moon, now hot sun, flashing green, yellow, orange and ochre, red, blue all around him, birds with sharp beaks and ripping claws. He laughed, floating swimming, perhaps even flying, in a boat, in the air, seeing crocodiles and sharks in the water ahead, this being dangerous country. There was weed-slime and stripped bone as well. This being cannibal country.

He clambered up mountains, through snowy ravines, under grey clouds and mist and bleached boulders. His shadow like ink on the sands at his feet, toes blistered and cracked trailing blood. There was death in the canyons, in the aquatic depths, in the cave mouths that loomed on either side. He laughed, floating swimming, defiant as he passed them, then glanced down a volcano at the crimson boiling lava, at the dragons and dinosaurs and primal fish. This reminder of origins, this horror.

Falling and tumbling, spiralling and flailing, his heart in his throat somewhere screaming. And beneath him the dragon's jaws, flames darting out, teeth as large as spears glistening greedily. A brief glimpse of fierce fire sucked into black depths, then a well plunging away to eternity. Somewhere another scream and a heartbeat like a gong and the world turning over, exploding. White stars, glowing moons, a collision of galaxies, rebirth in a womb in a bubble-car. Smiling hello to a brother long dead leering back with foam drool on the lips. Welcome, farewell, the Aztecs are coming. To this terrible territory in this great deep.

Temples in golden light, virgins enraptured, and blood on starched sheets between spreading thighs. The sacrificial lamb with a dagger at its throat bleating into the face of a killer-priest. Him you me us. Standing in silk robes on a sunblasted plain with his member straight out and engorged. The rhythms of worship, the multitudes howling, hands black against the white of a fierce sky. Wilderness, garden, deep river and sea, then a smooth swoop through inky inner space. This being an infinite country. There were atomic explosions and meteorites as well. This being elemental country.

He tripped between tonsils, slid down a windpipe, then fell into huge beating lungs. Rainbows through grey light, a harsh roaring storm, dimensionless chaos on all sides. He flew up and fell back down, flattened out and turned around, was sucked in and spat out of whirlpools. No heat, no cold, no night, no day, no heaven, no hell, no purgatory. He saw a line of white crosses running back to the horizon, a pillar of fire climbing high. He was frightened and exultant and helpless. He was chained to the rock.

Blood splashed on the rubbish, cats howling in heat, one hand up her skirt groping blindly. I love you I need you oh fuck God I'm hard in the breathless and tormenting adolescent night. He was down on his knees with his tongue up inside her, which he never had done in real life. Skirt over his head, sweat slick on her thighs, strands of hair at his nose breathing desperately. I love you I want you I need you oh Christ with the alley running away into black night. Long ribbons of darkness and pale-yellow light from the lampposts on pavements rain-drenched. Pedestrians like zombies, eyes thyroidal and glazed, not speaking stepping out of their tombs. Sky in convulsion, bombs falling on the ruins, the wailing of the lost and lamented. This being a world war and so forth.

He met Jesus, Judas, Nero, Napoleon, Hitler, Churchill, Chaplin, Valentino, Billy Cotton, Bing Crosby, Harold Wilson, Sydney James and the late great Anthony Aloysius. He toured Babylon, Damascus, Jerusalem, Cairo, Marrakech, Madrid, Paris, Peking, a city of rivers, an empire of slaves and Atlantis sinking into the sea. He broke bread for the hungry, wept wine for the thirsty, and was nailed to a cross pissing blood. He spoke in many tongues, dressed in rags and riches, died twice and was thrice resurrected. He was a man of many means, after all.

Snow on the mountain peaks, sun-bleached ancient ruins, forest fires burning up whole hills. Dense clouds, clear skies, splitting stars, dying suns, and the ghosts of the dead throughout the universe. In ravines, through jungles, up cliffs, across deserts, on oceans and verdant grasslands. His father, his mother, all the faces of his history floating in a fog in a dead dawn. He went out to infinity, to where the past meets the present, and he stayed there, enfolded, a witness.

Wheels spinning spinning-wheels spinning tapestries of time, the circular ruins of existence. First birth and final death, first creation and then destruction, cities rising and collapsing on the instant. He saw dust on the doomed stone, blood on the burnished brick, whole countries whose streets were all empty. He travelled. He moved. Seeing bottomless black pits and deep pockets in space and galaxies cascading over galaxies. Seeing sinners and saints, the living and the dead, all the ages of man within himself. Smelling songs, hearing colours, sensing skeletons in closets, seeing human heads sitting in egg-cups. And it being the feasting time of the festive season he partook and was cleansed of his guilt. He travelled on. He moved on.

He awoke.

Chapter Six

This hot noon. Of this intoxicated Sunday. Rising painfully with blood behind the eyes. Which blink reflecting sunlight from the window. Silvery incandescent. In other words, truly murderous. As the postman stands groggily beside the bed of the wife. Which is stained with recent sweat but no sperm. It being that lust does not reside here. Though it does in the boudoir of the widow Peggy Hartnett. Who last night did show him a plain bit of loving. Quickly over but immemorial. For the casual beauty of it. And the pure enthusiasm. Something we do not get in this forlorn house. This particular day nor any other.

-For Christ's sake! Your lunch! It's getting cold!

The voice of the soulmate. Ringing upward from downstairs. About as loving as the hands of a hangman. Now bawling about food. When the stomach is uneasy. After whiskey, beer and sausage. And much straining of the groin. Between sheets of an impeccable cleanliness. And thighs of mature strength and holding skill. In-out, up-down, gasp-groan, quiver, finish. Then spine to spine. Arses lovingly touching. Sleeping a sleep filled with fantastic dreams. Of brothers long gone and young ladies now hags. Of caves like vaginas and the boundless universe. Which just goes to prove that artistic thoughts. Linger there in the back of the brain-box.

-Get out of yer bed, for Christ's sake!

Refuse to reply. Such crudeness such bawling. To which we will not give in. Particularly on this sacred day. Of the Lord. Who protects us from ill. And forgives us our sins. Which are many and varied. Because of life's temptations. Weak mortals that we are. And of course that I am. Now pushing down the stiff cock and zipping up the trousers thinking Jesus it's noon and I'm thirsty. This being a fact of some considerable relevance. To the previous evening's debauchery with its violence and theft. And the quick poke that left us exhausted.

-Are you ready yet?

-Yes, dear.

-Jesus Christ!

Such blasphemy. From her lips. And on such a day too. When she should be on her knees in that church along the road. Head bowed and prayer dripping from her lips. Saying praise be to God for all He has given me. Not least a husband. Of the utmost gentility. Now tucking in his shirt. And padding down on bare feet. Corns on the toes on the carpet on the stairs. Leading into this small gloom. Of flowery wallpapered walls. And much abused furniture. None of it new. As I am frequently reminded. By the wife when we fight about money. And other sordid materialistic matters. Such being human nature. Base at its best. Which you cannot deny when you see the kitchen table. Surrounded by beasts tearing roast beef with their teeth. Gravy on their chins and much dribbling in industrious silence.

-Good family, good day to you.

-My God! In bare feet! And the smell!

-My dear wife, you're unkind. This unravelled day.

-Are you still drunk?

-Never was.

-Hmph.

Nose points at the ceiling, eyes roll in her head. A soggy lump now sweaty from the kitchen. Where she slaves for my welfare. But now drumming fingers on the table. Seated facing the daughter. The latter dressed in a dressing-gown draped loosely about her revealing a pink brassier and pimpled breasts. A shameless young creature. Who cares little for the brother who sits quietly beside her. Picking at potatoes and peering at a newspaper. One of the popular self-righteous dirty ones. Scandals galore for the hypocritical Sunday reader. Who wants God in one hand, a bit of dirt in the other. Revelations of sin mixed with piety and retribution. And gets it. In full. Page after sordid page. Bold headlines and black-and-white pix. Whores and pop stars. Pimps and politicians. Bare bums, big tits, long legs and blacked-out pubes. With editorials asking what can be done about it. When they're flogging it to death for all it's worth. And it's certainly worth a good read over the Sunday meat.

-I am seated. You may all begin to eat.

-Ha!

-Some joke!

-You 'ave a nerve!

Ignore them. These usurpers. Who take me for granted. As I pick up my utensils and gnash together the sound molars. Licking the lips with theatrical relish. Before tucking in to my roast beef and cabbage. With potatoes and carrots on the side. And my daughter's long legs crossed. Truly teasing to the right. Of the son who pretends to be reading. But is possibly tormented by incestuous thoughts. Which he cannot understand. As he flips over pages of multitudinous words. Thus creating a slight breeze that blows into my face. Cooling the hot food. As my jaws open wide. To swallow it down past the throat to the guts. Where it turns into putrescence. Which translated means shit. And comes out of the arsehole on the white-plastic seat. With much grunting and groaning to accompany it.

-The miracle of life indeed.

-What's that?

-I said, the miracle of life, dear. This food. One of your most treasured talents.

-Are you being sarcastic?

-I am not.

-Hmph.

So it goes. Domestic conversation. Spiritual rapport. The delightfully delicate despair of modern married life. Now, here, at this typical Sunday lunch. Son steeped in sordid scandals. Wife thinking evil thoughts. Daughter picking her teeth looking sensuous in a slovenly way. While the postman-father who delivers the Queen's mail delivers decent grub to his nauseous guts. Thus soaking up the booze. And the familiar morning sickness. Wiping satisfied lips with the back of a worker's hand. Ignoring the suspicion. In the eyes of the missus. In the head that swivels toward us with furrowed brow. It being that we didn't arrive home until this morning. Having said we spent the night with Mister Murphy after having a skinful.

-Are you finished?

-I am, sweet.

-Don't you sweet me.

-My apologies.

-Just hand me that plate and I'll be off.

-Why don't you just leave it? Rest awhile.

-And who's going to do the kitchen-work? You?

-No, thanks.

Thought she had me there but she hadn't. This hung-over gent being quick-witted still. While reaching out for a newspaper. Which opened hides the face. Pursing lips deep in thought. Studying international strife. And delicious national scandals. As she returns to the kitchen to once more wash the dishes. Sighing with despair as her fat arse rocks and rolls. In the face of our son who is scratching his balls. Distractedly. Adolescent and agitated. When threatened by the boobs in the News of the World. Which illustrate a feature about the need for moral rectitude. Something I doubt that my teenage daughter has. Her breasts bulging from her brassiere. Brazenly showing the red bite-marks. Of a male who ignores dental hygiene. It being that the teeth belong to that lout Briggs. Who chain-smokes cigarettes and lacks honourable ambitions. So. I should advise her. But how does one go about it? One opens the mouth and clears the throat and lets the words keep the phlegm down.

-My dear child.

-Who? *Me*?

-Yes, daughter. You. Please retire to your room and get dressed.

-Why? Do I bother you?

-It's not this family I'm worried about. It's your adolescent friends. Who could possibly arrive at any moment so please do what I say.

-Ah, Christ!

-Don't blaspheme.

-Oh, Jesus!

Hold rigid the line of this strong paternal jaw. Encourage no more insolence from the upstart. Who believes she is a cut above the rest of us. As she pushes back her chair and blushes and glares. Lips pouting and spine curved enticingly. Before flouncing up the stairs. Hips swaying as she disappears into the bathroom. To splash a handful of water on her all too willing flesh. Experienced in those ways that remain alien to our son. Who is, in his way, unusually innocent. Of lust's less endearing demands. Now ruffling his brown hair with restless fingers. Saying:

-Cor! There ain't 'alf some carryings-on!

-You are reading?

-The News of the World.

-An excellent journal.

-Too right.

Sighs with honest envy. Then changes the paper for the Mirror. Which I give him before burying myself. In line after line of typographical stimulation. Such as crime doesn't pay but isn't it fun? And how can we rid the country of the filthy pornographers who sell the disgusting pix we show here? Not forgetting the incest, prostitution and drug-addiction. With murder tucked away in some insignificant back column. Being one of the least shocking of Man's many vices. In a society that floats in a steamy sea of self-righteousness. A subject which the wife is not shy of discussing. Wiping hands and taking a chair by the table.

-What time's that film on the telly, then?

-Three.

-God, hours yet!

Her fat fingers outspread on the newspaper on the table. Some on Edward Heath and the others on Yoko Ono. With a thumb in the navel of a famous nubile actress. Who is being accused of behaving indecently in Knightsbridge. In a flat with some other famous friends having fun and fine feelings. Until the police sirens wailed. And the Law rushed in with some lucky photographers. Who will make a mint out of the exposure.

-Ought to be publicly horsewhipped.

-Pardon, dear?

-That crowd. Them film stars and the like. Gallavantin' about the way they do. Not an ounce of decency among the lot of 'em. Only the rich and famous can get away with it.

-But they didn't. They were caught.

-And what about all them poor wimmen? Raped by that sex-fiend in Fulham. Exposing it first. Then tryin' to stick it in 'em. He should be castrated, the beast.

-Possibly just sick, dear.

-I'm sure. And what about that one that made her livin' by strippin'? What about her, then? A famous man's daughter and she drags his name through the mud like that. Takin' off her clothes for them degenerates in Soho and tellin' it like all of us should try it. Six months in Holloway's what *she* needs.

Avidly turning more pages. Licking her lips. This Day of the Lord passing judgement. On the innocents whose blood is soaked up in these pages. Being read in countless millions of British homes. This very minute. By the silent majority. The new affluent working classes. With their cars, televisions and dish-washing machines. TV being the only one I permit in this house. Where old principles prevail and male chauvinism runs riot. Refusing to encourage lazy habits in the missus. Who scrubs clothes with her bare hands. Does the shopping on Shank's Pony.

And is grateful for the luxury of the fourteen-inch telly. Which she got by giving up her night of Bingo.

-Time?

-Film time.

-Thank God for that.

A romantic melodrama about a dying Scottish soldier. Played by Richard Todd for all it's worth. Which must be a lot. Since it's been on countless times. At least three times a year with the tears flowing out. Of women's eyes up and down the country. While the men. Like myself. Squirm in embarrassment. Or fall into bored slumber. Half-asleep half-awake. Wanting a shit but too lazy to get up and go. To the bog at the top of the stairs. Down which the daughter now sweeps with hips swaying. Dressed in hot-pants, thigh-boots and a red-hot skin-tight sweater. Bleached blonde hair tumbling over false black eyelashes. Above lips painted a phosphorescent pink. Handbag slung from one bare arm. Defiant.

-I'm going out.

-Oh?

-For a walk.

-Oh?

-Do you mind?

-Not at all.

-I'm surprised.

And out through the front door. To this sunny Sunday. And the local park where she'll meet up with the untrustworthy Briggs. While I recline here. In this chair with legs outstretched. Newspaper spread on the belly bloated with food. Which should be forced out. Through the magical anal passage. Something that one's stupor now prevents one from doing. This late mid-afternoon. The TV telling tales. Of a highly emotive nature. Inciting sadness in the wife. Derision in the son. And a definite discomfort in this old heart of mine. Talk of death, even cheap talk, reminding me of the past. Parents dying choking years apart, taking turns with TB. And one brother in the war. Falling on foreign soil. For King and Country. And the salvation of undeserving sods.

-Oh, God! Poor man! He's dying!

She's seen it a dozen times and always acts as if she's seeing it for the first time. Knuckles buried in her mouth eyes aglow. Son Ross collecting his jacket and slipping out quietly. Leaving mum and dad alone. With this flickering screen. And those ghost-like figures in this gloom-gathering room. With its past and present and future rolled into one. Brother dead and brother dying. Myself being the latter. Getting on in years and feeling the brittle bones. As they creak and ache. Sometimes moaning in the night and suffering dread in the heart. Tormented by a fantasy that has lately become recurrent. Of being buried alive being paralysed not dead. Dark suffocation and the rising mercy of madness. Rats nibbling at the arse. Worms wriggling in the mouth. Screaming please God release me though tongueless and dumb. And even now thinking about it. Recalling the awful dream. A bleak reminder of mortality. To be stringently avoided. Most of all when you have this increasingly bad cough. Hopefully to pass away in the next day or two.

-Oh, that was lovely. Really lovely. That poor, poor man. Dyin' like that. And bein' so brave about it.

-It was just a film, dear.

-It was glorious. That poor man broke my heart.

What do they hide behind their middle-aged masks? These ageing housewives and mothers with their bodies all wrecked. And no longer in need of the men who destroyed them. Just cooking and washing. Drifting aimlessly about. With only dreams to sustain them. Of the past and the future. Both better than the present. Both being unreal. Where lust does not enter and boredom does not exist. And where love lingers on ever after.

-He can act. Oh, he can act! He brings tears to your eyes.

-A heartfelt performance.

-Sarcasm. Trying to spoil it for me. Because you didn't like it yourself. A brute like you, perfectly understandable. God, what a life!

Goes back to the kitchen. To the dirty pots and pans. Still there while I sleep. Still reclining in this chair. Still there when I awaken and climb these steep stairs for a shit in this single small room. Cream walls cracked white pot. Chain with handle to pull. Linoleum on the floor beneath the bare feet curled downwards. Sending tingles up the calves to the thighs to the groin. Which would certainly excite were it not for the straining. Of bowels reluctant to release their heavy load. Though eventually giving in. With a plop and a splash. And deep sighs of relief from the lungs.

Time passes indifferently. This forlorn man with trousers. Around the ankles while the arse is steeped in thought. Doing this crossword. Puzzle of the week. Brow furrowed in stenchless concentration. Fourteen across fucks up twenty-three down and throws us back into confusion. Austria, Australia, Andorra, Auckland. None of those but how nice to go travelling. To such places. Palm trees and Bacardi. Loin cloths and lush tits. Strumming ukuleles on the white sands in the hot sun. Surf crashing onto the beach leaving small fish to eat. A healthy, hedonistic life. Far from the maddening crowd. It being that it's going back to nature. And all that bullshit.

Time's up. As the saying goes. When the show is over. And you have to leave. Ripping off this soft paper and wiping the backside. Not quite as hygienic as the Indian method but good enough for we Western barbarians. Then hitching up the trousers. And tightening the belt. Around the waist that still doesn't require braces. One hand on the chain. Which is expertly tugged. Deep thoughts on the infinite as water pours down. A catastrophe to ants and all microscopic life forms. A universe exploding by the Lord's righteous hand. Before He leaves this small room. The smallest room in the house. And closes the door carefully behind Him and goes back down the stairs. Sinking back into his armchair in front of the TV. Now turned off, thank

God.

-I tell you, I'm worried about that girl.

-Pardon, dear?

-Stop trying to sound like Noel Coward.

-My apologies. I didn't quite –

-Your daughter -

-Get you.

—needs a good talking to.

-Please, dear. Not now. I'll miss the news.

Cannot bear to be lumbered with paternal responsibilities. So turn on the telly and give it our full attention. The daughter needs talking-to. For her promiscuous ways. And someone should surely do it. Anyone but me. Who would die with embarrassment. At the very mention of the subject. Forced to say don't let him in there when I know that he has been. In there more than once. The immoral young lout. She having let him. The immoral young whore. Who also happens to be my daughter. Once beloved but now frightening in the beauty of her maturity. And in her cool, hard knowledge. Taking all she can get before the axe falls. To chop off her freedom and joy and thus make her respectable.

-You never want to talk about it. You always go deaf when I mention it. What kind of dad do you think you are? If that's not asking too much?

-The girl's old enough to look after herself.

-She's too old for her age and you know it. But alright, don't you worry, just don't think about it. But don't try blaming me when her belly swells and she wants to know what went wrong.

-I won't.

-No, you won't. You won't care a bugger. Or you'll want to beat her brains out.

-*Please*, dear. It's the news. It's important. I can't hear a thing.

Malodorous malpractices in the world beyond these walls.

W.A. Harbinson

Flickering bright on the screen square in front of glazed eyes. Bombs in Belfast, British hostage shot dead, and perhaps a second Bangladesh bloodbath. The evening's entertainment beginning in fine style. The Evolution of Man at first hand. Pollution, famine, rape, murder, genocide. And where would we be if we didn't have one another? Closer to peace than we are at this moment. Which I might actually believe were it not for the pictures. Violence and gore in full-colour close-ups. Speeches, insults, fanatical chanting and screaming. Politics broken up by advertisements and previews of the glories to be shown later on. The miracle of TV. Bringing the whole world to your doorstep. Life in the raw in the living room. Leaving you senseless.

-Look at him! The rotten liar! The parasitical bastard! What does *he* know about the working classes? The filthy-rich git!

-He has nice teeth.

-They're false.

-Please, dear. That's for his dentist to say.

She gives a raucous laugh and goes off to make some tea. Returns still visibly quivering with mirth. A religious programme has quickly come and gone, a weekly soap is mercifully winding down. Cup of tea in one hand, cheese sandwich in the other, this being sustenance for the evening ahead. Not to be lived truly. Merely quietly passed through. In a trance of boredom engendered by that flickering squawking screen. Folk-singing and dancing as the darkness descends. Us watching half-asleep. Half-awake almost numb. Responding only to vibrations. In the atmosphere. Making us resemble the living-dead.

-I love American musicals. They're so jazzy.

-Howard Keel and Betty Hutton. Such wonders.

-Alright, grumpy you. Just you be sarcastic. But *some* of us know how to relax.

-I'm relaxed to the point of rigor mortis.

-Then go out to the pub and get pissed again.

We would if we could but we can't. Being still a little ill

from yesterday's debauch. And being not quite as young as we were not long ago. The bones aching more readily. The stomach heaving with less excuse. Not forgetting the dizziness and tightness in the chest. Possibly psychosomatic. Or so my dictionary informs me. When I anxiously turn its pages to find out why I feel ill. Thus making myself feel guilty. Over my pitiful, mortal fears. And immortal self-pity. Which shoots lightning bolts from the brain to the nerves of the flesh. Causing self-induced pains and odd twitches and severe depression. Which I *do* tend to suffer. Heroically silent. And more often than not as of late.

    -David Frost soon. I could die.

    -Teeth. All teeth.

    -But not false.

    -An upper-class twit.

    -But so charming.

    -Well, in truth he's just middle-class, the twit.

    -You're just jealous, that's all. You're so dull.

    Perhaps I am. When viewed from the outside. The wonders of the interior not noticed. But very much alive here in magical me. Broad at the shoulder. Narrow at the hip. Bona fide teeth now well practised at biting. Erotically. In a juvenile way at this late great stage. Of a life that has not yet surrendered to final defeat.

    We are trembling this very second. With the silent mirth of the defiant. Sitting facing the wife whose cunt we once possessed. To make a metaphorical point to make a son. To make a daughter. To make love when it was novel and we were fit and had the faith of the foolish. A long time ago. For a brief melting time. Before boredom set in and gradually drained us dry. Of affection or the means of expressing it. Though I'm still not sure which.

    -Have another cup of tea before it starts.

    -So kind, my dear. So thoughtful. You make my heart sing.

    -You say that, I sometimes want to believe you.

-Believing costs nothing.

The offspring are still out. Walking the lamplit streets. Or licentiously embraced. Under the stars. Or in the rear seat of a car. God knows and looks down in forgiveness. We hope. As we sit here. In this dwindling Sunday. With the TV flickering. Lots of snow on the picture. As the news is repeated. All bad as it should be. Private vice and public violence. Sexual shenanigans and general mayhem. With spaceships to Mars travelling on unmolested. Leaving us with our Earthly concerns. So pathetically mundane. Such as how do we live with the debris of our existence? Such as wives and sons and daughters. And the many deceits.

-Your tea.

-Thank you, dear. Most considerate.

-There's David! Oh, God, he's so charming!

Teeth gleaming. Eyes shining. Oily charm in the voice. This idol of the spastic plastic age. Turning middle age to transient beauty and deceptive girlishness. Her pale cheeks suddenly glowing. Her chin resting on folded hands. Elbows propped up on the knees in this deepening gloom. Undisturbed by the daughter who sneaks through the front door and then up to her bedroom looking guilty. Followed ten minutes later by the gangling son who slumps into an armchair looking bored. Unreal at this late hour. Another ghost in a shadowed corner. Slipping and sliding through the increasingly disjointed thoughts. Which creep quietly from this room. And crawl wearily up the stairs. And slip into the bed and sleep snoring in the form of the real man.

-Waken up! Move over! Great lump that you are! Takin' up all the space as usual.

-What? Good God! My sweet angel.

-Oh, yeah? Who's *you* dreamin' about, then?

Amused mockery in her voice. But also some affection. As she turns her back to me. Her vast arse at my belly. And expects me to press. Tighter to her for the warmth. Which graciously I do. One arm looping across her. Its hand falling upon her breast. Which is warm and not surprisingly soft and makes me feel at peace. And then desolated. Suddenly swept with waves of sadness and fear. As emotional as a child and not understanding why. Pressing lips to her spine. Closing eyes to search for solace. Recalling years gone by and other nights spent together. Hopelessly helpless and drowning in love. Which sweeps us from this sheltering harbour.

Into chaos.

Chapter Seven

He slept.

And went down the dark tunnel through the white whipping lights through a hot blaze of stars in an inky deep. There was infinite night and an uncoiling flame that flared red to haze purple horizons. He fell into the sea that reflected the black sky, into sludge-slashed waves and a howling wind. The soaked rock beside him, looming out of the mist, was his anchor and sole source of comfort. He kicked frantically, swimming, slapping desperately at the foam, and was sucked into murmuring depths. There was dread and suffocation and much screaming. There was pain without end.

He laughed rising high, released and exultant, arms spreading to embrace the dawning day. Cocoons of fluffy cloud and smooth sheets of sheer blue over widening flatlands ribbed with rivers. Three humans in a huge jug of gleaming glass splashed in sunlight reflecting their wild eyes. The jungle below, throbbing drums and pagan rites, with the bloody dagger drawn from ear to ear. A lurch and sudden spinning, a dissolving into chaos, then the laughter of ghosts in the ether. Then abruptly the forest floor, dense foliage and gloom, motes of dust at play in shimmering air.

Harsh chatter striking terror to the breast.

The two primeval beasts fighting, teeth exposed rending flesh, leaving white bone revealed through crimson blood. Towering up to the trees, razor-sharp claws at his nose, lumps of torn fur and entrails at his feet. The growls from their throats like the elements at war, his heart pounding like a huge gong gone mad. Lying in the hole far beneath looking up as the guts splashed all over the window-pane. Worms and large spiders and centipedes too, in the mouth, in the ears, at the anus. Screaming please God have mercy and then fleeing, heart pounding, eyes sightless.

On his knees he was worshipping.

The temple soared high from the weeds to the clinging vines hazed in a silvery spray of moonlight. Above it the pale lunar eye coldly staring, beneath it the multitudes praying. Black heads in the turbans wrapped in togas above the sandals with the toes touching mud and muddied bark. Somewhere the drums and the alien rhythmic chanting and the hypnotic snout of the snake. Then the blade of the dagger drawn from ear to bloody ear on the throat of the virgin on the altar. Black blood on white marble, a brief throttled groaning, disembowelment, then dessert on the innards.

Heart, lung and kidneys. Great stuff.

Wiping the lips with the tongue of a corpse, drinking piss from a whore's hidden hole. Pick the teeth with a hot cock and clean hands in shit before moving on trailing clouds of gold-dust. Garlands of flowers leading down to the white beach now burned by the heat of the noon sun. In the sands under palm trees, surf arching above the shore, lush breasts over loincloths on honeyed thighs. The men without arms playing banjos with their teeth in tents supported by sharks' jaws propped open. Native hands at his balls cupping geysering sperm. A Union Jack raised on his stiff member.

Lying back, feeling free, he surrendered.

In the train in the tunnel through the mountains to the plains where the parched rock and cacti awaited him. Three men around a black pot of white-foaming golden beer stirring and stamping feet on hot coals. Faintly familiar and frightening too, stony lunacy brightening their wide eyes. Cackling insanely and starting to flee, seeing wilderness dust change to metal. Smooth cold and shiny stretched out to the horizon where the huge silver blades turned on great wheels. A million men buried to their necks in the sea of steel screaming dementedly with almighty terror. And the silver blades spinning to chop off their heads by the thousands with blood flooding the plain.

He went back to the arena and stood beneath God with the crowd roaring displaying their admiration. And Nero, who was present, placed a rose in his navel and sent him on home with a smile

through the infinite void, the inky deep.

to the primitive village, to the thatched shacks on stilts, to the cannibals stewing the missionaries. The screaming of a woman being boiled alive slowly with her brassiere ripped off incidentally. And floating in the human soup one pair of spectacles supporting two noses propped upright. One eye staring out from a grill of mixed fingers and thumbs, a salad of testicles and pubic hair.

He stood by the spit having come to the rescue regardless of natives painted and feathered. Butchered torsos to the fore, severed heads to the rear, a tongue wriggling up his right leg like a fat worm. He stood with no trousers and his impressive cock thrust out like a tree trunk horizontally aligned. Bloated and blue-veined, energetically quivering, it ran toward the bush like a highway. And seated on stools on either side of this wonder the natives were nibbling at pink flesh. Not painful but frightening and ultimately impossible. He blacked out and awakened to dazzling light

blazing over the wilderness, the boundless parched plains, the cacti and dead dust and scorched bones. And swaying on a rock the mottled neck of a snake spitting hissing at shimmering air and clouds of fat flies. Much buzzing and squawking and slithering in the sand, with the stripped bones of three men now faceless.

World's End, desolation and glazed sky high above with the wind howling spectrally through gullies. Featureless and flat running out to the horizon out of which emerged one lonely speck. Imperceptible at first but growing larger every second coming toward him from a silvery haze. He clambered to his feet and ran away from the hollows gouged out of the dirt by his bruised knees. And ran to the figure stumbling brokenly towards him in tattered rags ringing a bell. Moaning and groaning, death rattle in his throat, bursting boils and flesh dripping from palsied limbs.

He stopped and stood frozen by this horror before him, this doomed man, this saviour in disguise. And he looked at the stoned eyes, at the trembling limbs, and then saw that this leper was himself.

He awoke.

Coughing.

Chapter Eight

A fine morning today. Crisp. The sky greyish-blue. Not yet brightened by sunshine. Fluffy cocoons of white cloud and birds circling gracefully. Above rooftops of black slate and telegraph wires shivering over streets still pleasantly supine. Before being battered by the rushing of booted feet. Those of the working classes. Up early to be checked in by punch-clocks and KGB superiors. Just like me, more's the pity.

Yet still taking pleasure from this early-morning hour. Always keen to be outside and busy going about my business. Which prevents introspective speculation. About subjects titillating or terrifying. Best to keep the beast at bay. Lest paranoia take over. So therefore not displeased to see this High Street post-office. Already opened and swept clean by the always nervous Missus Grimsby. Who has been our charlady for almost fifteen years. And suffers sundry complexes about intimate matters. About which we tease her to make her blush bright-red. Saying some day we'll buy her a pair of pink knickers. With a lover's heart stitched over the appropriate area. This being an idea which certainly appeals. As we waltz lightly in here. Singing a merry song. To see her glance up from beneath the wooden counter. Where on hands and knees she scrubs the tiled floor.

-Morning, Missus Grimsby. And a lovely one it is. Almost as attractive as the generous spread of posterior that you're so kindly showing me. A satisfying sight.

-Oh, you devil! You wicked brute! What a thing to say!

95

Never known the likes of you! And never want to again, goodness gracious!

Springs to her feet. With an energy that belies her grey hair and considerable weight. Being a matronly figure with matching personality. Sentimental as they come and constantly reading Mills & Boon romance novels. Believing everything written in them. Forever sighing and whispering how sweet. With tears in her eyes. And a bit of sniffing as she wipes the tears away. Doubtless thinking of her teenage daughters. About whom she constantly worries. Imagining dirty old men like the Postie creeping toward them under cover of darkness. Though managing to forget that concern when I crack a joke or two. Thus managing to make her chuckle. While keeping a safe distance between us. Which she needs because of her strong belief in the matrimonial bonds. About which I am not bothered even though she thinks them sacred. So I merely pinch her backside. Now and then to hear her squeal. With embarrassment *and* pleasure, I'm sure. Though naturally she tries to hide the latter.

-Dear Missus Grimsby. When you blush you're beautiful. As you are this very moment. But beware. Because I feel a growing attraction for you. And some fine day might not be able to control myself. And will hurl myself at you with the worst of intentions. To enthral or disgust you.

-Deary me. If my husband could only hear you now.

-A lucky man, Missus Grimsby. No doubt about it. I only hope that he appreciates what he has. And is hopefully getting.

-Now you *stop* that, Postie! You're getting me all flustered and putting me off my work. And I have to be finished in twenty minutes. I've never *known* the likes of you!

-Eliza, dearest, would you like a cup of tea? For the warmth it will provide. With a biscuit to keep up the strength without adding on more weight.

-Oh, you *are* a kind man. Beneath all that bluster. I'm sure you keep your own wife in a spin, day in and day out.

-That I do, Eliza. Treat her like a queen. With tenderness

and good humour. Thus preserving the love of earlier years. If not actually increasing it.

-Yes, you're really a romantic at heart. I can tell that. I mean, all that wicked talk aside.

-Cut this tongue out, dear lady.

Into this tea-room of stained cups and saucers. Switch on the electric kettle and place biscuits on a plate. For the nourishment of Grimsby. Who if knowing how I really treat the missus would undoubtedly be bitterly disillusioned. Though this cannot stop me wondering. What the old dear is like. In bed with her man who should have passed on years ago. Being like the living dead. A shocking judgement on my part. Encouraging me to go about other business. While the kettle is working itself up to its whistling climax.

Sprightly out this door and in through another. The cosy office of the Senior Postmaster. Named Mister Fish. And certainly smells accordingly. Being a despicable creature, mean-eyed and moustachioed. Conceived in a computer. Umbilical cord of red tape. Knowing only the language of the Rule Book and tormenting us with it.

Vengeance is mine, said the Lord. So reach down with the right hand. Behind this wooden cupboard. To disconnect Mister Fish's Very Important Telephones. Because being an idiot he'll be frustrated for hours. Before thinking to look. For the obvious. So likewise this toilet-seat. His very own and almost holy. Grinning sadistically as I smear the seat with Lysol. Which should give him a hot arse for a considerable period of time. Then back to the whistling kettle. Letting the eyes fill up with sadness. For the benefit of Missus Grimsby. Who being romantic will imagine things. And now pour this fine brew and then take it out to her. With a smile to make the sad eyes heart-wrenching when she ponders my secret grief.

-Eliza, please. Sit here and talk to me. Nor normally enough time in this busy world for such civilised activities. Yet surely necessary. Since conversation is even better than television. Or even a good game of darts.

-I'll just sip my tea as I work, thanks. I've lots to do and not much time to do it. If Mister Fish comes in and finds me lagging there'll be hell to pay.

-You worry too much, Eliza. Life is too short to be wasted on such pointless anxiety. And Fish will end up just like you and me. In a nice long brown box.

-You're a bold one, alright. Sitting there when you should have already filled your mailbag. Some day he'll sack you, mark my words. You *know* you go out of your way to antagonise him.

-The man is a pompous buffoon with delusions of grandeur. Small brain, hard heart and as tight as a drum. No compassion, Eliza. No understanding of human frailty. And it's not being married that did it to him. Festering frustrations, don't you know? Leaving nothing but bitterness.

-Well, now, I'd rather not discuss that subject. Some things are too private.

Rest the arse on this counter with the uniformed legs crossed. Nonchalance in the pose. Good humour in the face. Cup and saucer balanced expertly in one hand while the other holds the half-eaten biscuit. Watching the poor slave scrub away there. Between anxious gulps of her tea. Since if the leper-faced Fish were to walk in right now Missus Grimsby would possibly shit herself. Heart pounding and nerves all ajangle. Like Fish's agitated balls. Unexercised, lo, these many years. Apart from shameful self-stimulation. Working with a quick hand and greedy, grasping fingers. In the dead of his guilty nights. When we would have liked to peek. Through a hole in the wall near his bed. To observe him leer at saucy pin-up pictures. Of the kind one will not tolerate in one's own home. Being of sound mind and healthy body. And high moral fibre.

Self-conviction must reign supreme. Lest the shocking truth slip out. Since, when we dwell on the sexual habits of others, we are forced to think of our own vices. As indeed we do too often. More so as of late. Vague disturbances in the thoughts which we

98

cannot quite define so if rich would go and see a psychiatrist. Stretch out on his comfortable couch. Let him pick this polluted brain for the filthy thoughts therein. To be recycled later in my highly personal memoir. An extraordinary treat for the literary world. Which is filled with trendy folk. Who would read the disgusting tome and chuckle. While Mary Whitehouse trembled. Grieving for the moral welfare of unborn generations. Exposed to the published perversions of a dirty old postman. Who is already feeling tired. Unusually so. Certainly more tired than normal. As he watches Missus Grimsby packing up to go home. To her unemployed husband. And virginal daughters. Who have often teased this postman during pavement encounters. With their ripe nubile flesh. And its promise of the unrestrained pleasures we all secretly dream about.

Now seek a little distraction by returning these cups and saucers. To the tea-room to quickly wipe them clean. Then back to pack the mailbag. Sorting the letters and packages into their respective streets. Deliberately industrious before the rest of the staff arrive. To greet me with smiles or perhaps the odd scowl. Depending upon personal dispositions.

-Morning, Mister Fish! A fine Monday for work! I'm already prepared to hit the road. So pleased to see that you've finally arrived.

He mumbles a reply deliberately inaudible. And stares at me with candid suspicion. Which scares me not at all as I gaze back with a bland smile. Causing his sneaky gaze to drop. From the sight of my bulging mailbag. Which is proof of my industry and validates my existence. Which each tied bundle destined for an individual street. And all the bundles combined representing my working world. Which is just about all of the world that I possess. Pitiful or grand, depending on how you look at it. And I not only look at it, but have to carry it on my back. To make the shoulder ache and further flatten flat feet. This being the price we have to pay to hold the world in our hands.

Still holding the bland smile. As I watch Mister Fish. While he inspects his cosy office with an air of disdain. Through which I can see with my keen X-ray vision. As he glances from the corners of his own mistrustful eyes. At me. Trying to work out exactly how long I've been in. And also why I am here so early. But the information booth is closed. Therefore unable to assist him. While I find myself thinking that some day I'll fix him properly. Though hot toilet seats and disconnected telephones will have to suffice for the present.

-Morning, Harry!

-What's good about it?

-Didn't say it was good. Merely mentioned the morning.

-Christ, *what* a morning! Head like a balloon, nausea in the guts, and shit pouring non-stop from my arse. Never again, amigo. The quiet life from now on. I'm going to turn to God or maybe become a Scientologist, and I'll never go back to Camden Town as long as I live. Irish Micks and pints of Guinness and whiskey chasers on the side. My God! So how went *your* weekend?

-Reasonable, Harry. No more, no less. Painted the kitchen for the wife. Fixed the TV for my son. Put new lino on the stairs and disciplined the daughter. Responsibilities, Harry. Being married, one can't avoid them. So one is, this morning, rather weary. Needless to say.

-If that speech was for the benefit of that pig, Fish, he's just gone to the bog.

-Thank you, Harry, for that helpful observation. I can see that no more breath need be wasted on you.

An admirable fellow. Who shares my singular loathing for the Senior Postmaster. Good old Harry, not related to Lime. Or Orson Welles. A clerk by day and a debauchee by night. When he tours the less salubrious watering-holes of lovely Camden Town. North London's very own little Soho. Where he seeks out ladies dressed in leather with metal studs. Who offer him whippings while bestriding him in spiked heels. Inflicting punishment. Of the kind that helps him unburden himself of his

100

heavy load. Such being the nature of his bachelor's perversions. Which I do not criticise. Being sensitive to human frailty. Something he appreciates and often kindly rewards. Such as the time he took me off for a game of lunchtime snooker. Claiming to be an amateur. Before taking me to the cleaners for ten of the crisp ones. Thereby robbing the missus of her expected bag of groceries. But claimed he felt guilty and offered me a local lady. Mentioning something about compensation. Saying take her three ways on the house in that bog out the back. An irresistible offer that I managed to resist. Having concern for the diseases that proliferate where sexual freedom prevails.

-Hey, Postie! *Postie*!

-Undivided attention, Harry.

-What's the matter with Fish? He's just come out of the bog. Red-faced and frantically scratching his arse. Also glaring at you.

-Must be worms, Harry. Could not be anything else. It's clear that Mister Fish never goes near a bath. Altogether a filthy creature, Harry. Of that I am certain.

-If it's worms, you put them there, you evil bastard. And some day, believe me, he'll catch you and make you pay for it.

-Fear not, Harry. I know my worker's rights. If he merely glares, it's his personal prerogative. But if he actually makes an accusation, it's victimisation. At which I shall promptly wave my trade union card.

-Yeah, right.

-No flies on this old soul. I well remember that last occasion. He found a dead dog's balls and penis in his pocket and instantly blamed me. Described me as a communist anarchist bastard. And called me other names too obscene to mention. I was appalled and deeply hurt. My sensibilities were wounded. I came close to reporting him, but finally refrained, determined to show that human decency could prevail over the base need for vengeance. So I let him off with a warning. And he's hated me ever since.

-I'll give you a soapbox.

-Not required, Harry. Honesty is all. The truth speaks for itself.

-Jesus Christ, what a windbag!

Sprightly through the front door comes Miss Emily Forthright. Bouncing bosom way ahead. Nipples visible through the blouse extremely tight around the waist above hot-pants. Tanning-lamp legs raised on high on stiletto-heeled boots. Which make one breathe deeply and almost groan when greeting her good morning. Resisting the urge to pinch her ripe rump. As she she-shays past widening male eyes to the door of that cupboard. Standing on tiptoe to hang up her coat. Stretching tendons in the legs sensually curved and corrupting. Leading up to twin mounds and the shadow of a crevice. Which we dare not dwell upon in this early-morning hour of this new day.

-Miss Emily, good morning.

-Christ, I'm whacked!

-Ah. Then the weekend was enjoyable.

-Christ, I don't think I can keep this up. Mad Mick on Friday, Smooth Steve on Saturday, and pitiful Paul home for supper on Sunday. Oh! And that rich cunt called Compton on Sunday morning. In church, I mean.

-An interesting departure. From the norm.

-Yeah. Too true. And what a drag. But Jesus, that smoothie Steve on Saturday night. What a *beast* he turned out to be! After the movies. A couple of gin-and-tonics in the pub next door. Generous with it, no question, but thought it gave him the right to dry his sweaty hands on my tits. Later in a bleedin' Mini Minor. Like a couple of acrobats! Almost wrecked him and certainly exhausted me. Finally hit him with my shoe, scratched his face with my fingernails, and told him to explain them to his wife when she saw his fresh scars.

-And then?

-Gave in, gave it. What else could I do? He looked so forlorn, so deprived, it just broke my heart. We got out of the car

102

and I put out in my flat and now I'm hurting like hell.

-You have heart, Emily. And a generous spirit. A rare and dying breed in this bleak age. Would you not care to extend such generosity to an old man in need?

-Aw, come *on*, Postie!

-I mean it.

-You don't.

-Alas, I hunger. For the loss of my youth and its helpful vitality. As I suffer in silence the sad decline of the years. And look forward glumly to the days of my old age. Which, even though they may be mellow, can only end in oblivion.

Many have dropped the lace knickers for less. And, having dropped the aforementioned, dropped all inhibitions. For quite amazing indeed is the power of vocabulary. And the tone of the voice. Not forgetting one's modest histrionic talents. Which can certainly work wonders. As we now observe them doing. As she visibly trembles. Breasts out sucking in her breath. And turns toward us the radiance of her bedybize eyes. Even more bedybize when verging on the tearful. Doubtless caused by her sympathy as she thinks of the dear Postie. Who is tragic but dignified and therefore rather lovable. Not knowing that he's a rogue on the quiet. Or would certainly like to be.

-Gee, Postie, I…

-No. Say no more.

Turning quickly aside. With a touch of the dramatic. Sighing as if at one's own funeral and facing it bravely. Leaving her to tremble. Wiping tears from her eyes. Pained and confused wondering was the Postie serious or not. Glancing sideways at him as he laboriously picks up his canvas mailbag. Taking the world onto his shoulders. The weight of the bag adding to his appearance of sad nobility. Not forgetting that maturity is attractive to the young. And can often make gains out of losses when the going gets rough.

Yet we cannot avoid the truth. That her very presence heightens one's feelings of loss. Thus giving rise to ribald comments. For the benefit of good friend Harry. That sordid sensualist now standing behind the counter. Staring at me in a way he has never done before. As if he had just seen a ghost on my shoulder. Which I sense sitting there as I leave through the side door. Suddenly feeling cold and haunted. Trying to shake the ghost off me as I turn left and raise the right hand. Shaking visibly as it drops a plain brown envelope into the Post Office mailbox. A fairly large bulky envelope. Containing pornographic pix. Which will now travel along official channels. Stamped, sealed and delivered. Straight to the unwitting hands of one who has tormented me. In the hope that his further education will give him a heart attack.

-Poor old Postie, there, he looked like a bleedin' ghost.

But along this lively thoroughfare. Humming a song to show defiance. A silvery-haired spectre in the sunlight breaking out through the dense clouds. Looking up at the brightening sky. At birds circling on high. Lowering the gaze to take in the human pageant spreading out all around him. Hearing the city's heartbeat. Smelling its petrol breath. Observing its multifaceted chaos in this promising morning. With a racing heart. And heightened anticipation. And with an odd, uneasy weariness that makes him cough nervously.

Chapter Nine

The postman's knock. Knock, knock. And no filthy remarks. Because I'm at it again. Waiting for the shiver of dusty curtains and the appearance of one large nervous eye. Neither manifestation being forthcoming. Which is odd. To say the least. It being that she has always been up at this time. Trembling with anticipation. Thus a slight chill here. Imagining all kinds of terrible possibilities. Such as suicide, rape or murder. With natural causes for death coming last in the thoughts.

So knock again. Knock, knock. While the precarious ticker races. Thus proving the humanity of this caring soul. Brimming over with pity and affection for the lonely Miss Eleanor Rigby. Also burning with embarrassment at the very possibility of being the one to discover the corpse inside. Man like myself being much too sensitive for such awfulness.

So knock a third time. Knock, knock. More firmly and louder than before. Bruising the knuckles and then stepping back a little. With shock. When the door swings open with unusual speed. To reveal the timid lady draped only in her dressing-gown. An unexpected sight. One might even say shocking. More so because her sad eyes are crimson. Matching her flushed cheeks.

-Oh, God, I'm drunk, but I love that man!

Stinking of whiskey and perhaps a dash of gin. And making statements that when sober would to her sound obscene. Cannot believe my eyes. Nor attune my ears to this new voice. The human brain, after all, can only take so much. Before it boggles.

105

As mine is doing right now. Since lunacy is clearly afoot here. The frustrations finally exploding. Thus behind her crimson eyeballs a real hint of menace. And possibly the rise of rapacity.

Am aware of my own attractions but never expected this. Certainly not from the timid soul, Miss Rigby. Who could be at me in a minute with greedy hands. Ripping the clothes from me crying yummee. Trying to bite it. If she can stoop that low long enough. Or focus her weepy peepers. Which formerly were crystal-clear. While I suffer shame in the knowledge that I've stepped away from her. And for once am rendered speechless. Something previously experienced only in special circumstances. Such as sex or sleep. With thoughts of the former now causing me to notice. The edge of a brassiere-strap. Under her dressing-gown. Sexy though confirming that something is amiss. Such as her reasoning. Which makes me shiver uncomfortably. Being a great one for dreaming. Of loonies who leer demonically in the delirium of the night. So now straighten the shoulders and make ready to run. In case she charges at me. With years of sensual hunger to be appeased.

-Nothing for you, Miss Rigby. Only knocked on the door to bid you a hearty good morning.

-Oh, God, I'm drunk, but I love that man!

Slam. Goes the door. Right in my face. As I blink the startled eyes and take note of my trembling. Accepting that it must have been real, after all. That very strange vision. Of Miss Rigby drunk in her dressing-gown at this ungodly hour.

Better get away fast. Before she changes her mind and comes back out. At full bore. At me. Who would die from embarrassment. And perhaps a little shame. Always having been one for taking the initiative. Where lust is concerned. Which thought helps my legs to move at an unusually lively pace. Though cannot recall when I began walking. Or how I reached where I am at this singular moment.

A lunchtime drink is clearly in order. Absolutely necessary. For the demented form of sanity that might be found there. At the bottom of an amber glass. Though notice that I'm still pushing letters through mailboxes. As usual. Thus proving that instinct is more durable than intelligence. Which I appear to lack at this crucial moment.

-Top of the morning to you, Missus Whittaker.

-Hmph.

-I say, Missus Whittaker! A hearty good morning to you!

-I want none of yer lip. With the likes of you the insults can be sensed even before they're spoken.

-A generous statement, Missus Whittaker. Warming this cold heart of mine. No mail for you today. Which is not really surprising. Since, as we both know, there rarely is.

-Meaning?

-That no one talks where there are no ears listening. That no one performs where no one is looking. That no one offers when there is no hope of thanks.

-Are you drunk?

-Not in the manner with which you are familiar.

-Then yer stupidity's showin'. You may think yer bein' smart, Mister, but them words don't mean a thing to man or beast.

-Man may ignore them; it's the beast that cannot understand. Now as our friends across the Atlantic would say: Have a good day.

And off with a zippy movement. As she screams to the rear. That she doesn't have to take insults. From a common shit of a postman. Who is whistling a happy tune. To let her know that she screams in vain. Ignoring these grubby *kinder* hopping noisily along the pavement. All distinctly resembling their awesomely awful mother. One of them a small girl. Black-smudged eyes glaring at me. Doubtless calculating some form of revenge on behalf of her mother. Not for one moment suspecting that I might get in first. By taking the firecrackers that she often pushes through Miss Rigby's mailbox. And tying them to the elastic of her cheap, unwashed knickers. Match flaring at the fuse. To ensure a bouncy performance. And much agitation. This doubtless being a childish notion. But possibly effective if carried out. And satisfying to old men turning senile in the morning's tentative sunlight.

Zippy indeed, but not too fast. Remembering to stop at this house for which a letter, certainly lewd, has been designated. Straight to loose Louise from her delinquent boyfriend. Who might one day be caught with his pants down. In the act. In a telephone booth. With a policeman hammering his knuckles on the glass pane of the door. Bellowing filth and fornication. In a magisterial tone of voice. Before ordering out that decadent delinquent. And inviting into the booth his slavering self. If I know the constabulary. Which I do believe I do. Friendly Constable Jim Rogers being one tarnished example. Confiding to me over beers that he once caught two teenagers. Hard at it under a tree in the darkness of Hampstead Heath. So sent the youth packing. But kept hold of the girl. Saying he wouldn't tell her mum. If she didn't tell her dad. It being highly unlikely that she would. After the kindly policeman had rogered her himself. Before walking her to safety as a gentleman should. Having turned her into a victim of her own sexuality. Just like loose Louise Bleakley. Who now stands in the doorway of her modest terraced house. Sweet breasts heaving as she sucks a swollen thumb.

-Miss Bleakley.

-Yeah.

-Bright is the flower in May, Miss Bleakley.

-It's not May.

-All the brighter that makes the flower.

-Gee, man, you're way out. You must listen to folk songs or something.

Folk songs indeed. Damned be the day that I attune these sensitive ears to such maudlin trash. Tits. And pert ones too. Are the reasons, my dear. If you did but know it. And I'll bet you do. In secret. Glowing inwardly with your feminine power. Which is dangerously attractive. To an old fool like the postman. Who hands her this envelope with a very fast hand. Lest she notice the trembling. An ailment that has lately come upon him. In the infirmity of his waning years. But still fit enough to be fascinated by the sight of her. Chewing on bubble-gum.

-From a lover, no doubt.

-Yeah. The creep.

And disappears inside. Looking anxious.

-Postman, Postman, bring me an aerogramme.

No time to dwell on a troubled teenage glance. For now on the pavement is the lovely Mary McKay. Whom I secretly adore. And whose soldier-husband is in Belfast dodging the bang-bangs. Fighting for his life. And hopefully with thoughts of her. Which is something I pray for. Even as I suffer another bout of coughing. Feeling relief only when it stops. Though anxiety lingers.

-Sorry, Miss Lovelorn, but nothing for you today. Except my unstinting adoration.

-Never on Monday. As well you know, Joe.

-My name isn't Joe.

-How do you know, Joe?

-My mother told me.

-She must have been pulling your leg. You *must* be a Joe, Joe. You *look* like Joe.

-Who's Joe?

-He's a gentle, fatherly man. In disguise. Not only gentle, but tired. Not only fatherly, but old. And wonderful for it.

-Sounds human.

-I'm mad about him, Joe.

-Tomorrow a letter. For sure.

She smiles and is gone. Along the street with her shopping bag. Loose skirt billowing up as she departs. Intoxicating to jaded eyes. Raised on high by her beauty. And her feminine frailty. So easily broken by the unexpected. Such as bad news from Belfast. My silent prayer being that I do not become the one who brings it. In the shape of an envelope with an MoD stamp. Containing news of her husband's untimely death. Courtesy of an IRA bullet. So I pray that it doesn't happen. Because a helpless coward am I when it comes to such matters.

Accepting this bitter truth as I cross the street. Walking a languid backward arc. Ignoring the house of the widow Peggy Hartnett. My partner in sin. But eventually stopping to knock. Knock, knock. Upon the door of the terminally unemployed Archie Brown. That amiable blood-sucker. Who caused a shocking riot on Saturday evening. Over drunken pride and free beers. Embarrassing me. When I was only too willing to pay for them and maintain the peace.

Such being one's nature. Sensitive. And often hurt by the harsh truth. That the sensitive must stand alone. In a world where love is rare and the gentle of heart a minority. Sincerely believing this as I knock on the door again. Just as it opens. Thus causing my knuckles to land on Archie Brown's nasal passages.

-Christ, my nose! You stupid berk!

Stepping back with one hand over his face. Tears in his red eyes. Which blink rapidly displaying mild shock. As he surfaces reluctant as always from sleep. To the dangers of the new day. Fingering his bruised proboscis with much sniffing and weeping.

-A thousand pardons, Archie. Accident unavoidable. As you can see. Where no door, thin-air. And the force of unhindered velocity. All missiles must land.

-Stupid, sterile, self-satisfied shit-head. What've you got for me this morning?

-Nothing.

-Then why the fuck did you knock on my door?

-To offer you the comfort of civilised conversation.

-Smart bastard. I can't see my bottle of morning sickness, meaning milk. Don't tell me you've pinched it.

-No more milk, Archie. I heard it on the grapevine. Meaning from the milkman direct to me. No money, no milk, he said, staring right at this door.

-The end has come.

-Indeed.

-I'll have to look for work.

-Correct.

-Life's becoming pure hell. And a bloody thief into the bargain. Tell me, Postie. How can you face it sober?

-With courage.

-And the exploitation of others. So where did you get to on Saturday night? When the shit hit the fan and the entertainment began?

-Touch of the old indigestion. Almost doubled me up with pain. But struggled gamely to the outer world. Where I stiffened the upper lip and suffered in silence. Sad at heart to have missed all the fun.

-You lying turd. Dodging out of it as always. Probably to go fuck that Peggy Hartnett. Piss off, you untrustworthy cunt.

Stepping unsteadily back inside. Slamming the door in my face. Leaving silence in this early-morning street. Along which I walk again. But not with great joy. Thinking of Peggy Hartnett. Legs apart me between them. Both pleased with our secret. Which seems to have swept the street. Archie Brown knowing. And mad Murphy also. With the eyes of Missus Whittaker not suspicious for nothing. Not to mention Hans Wernher who raised the subject the other day. And who this second sits on the doorstep straight ahead. Unaware of the pornographic pictures in the post. Which he should receive this afternoon. When they are dropped into the sorting-machine and pop out the other end. Officially stamped and rendered legal. All set to be innocently unwrapped and drive him frantic with lust.

-Top of the morning, Mister Wernher. You look as happy as ever. Seated on the doorstep with your vile thoughts illuminating your corrupt face.

-Happiness is the fancy of children and old men. Such as your pitiful self. Kindly keep walking and take your supposed happiness with you. It offends me and stinks in God's nostrils.

-You're familiar with God?

-I converse with Him at night. In the darkness of my thoughts. When I'm in a condescending mood. He's a gross megalomaniac who has failed to impress me. And so I can scorn Him. Infinite wisdom doesn't create the kind of world we live in. You loathe my cynicism, but this filthy life caused it. The world is God's toilet, my friend, and we are His shit.

-You see only one side of life. You choose to ignore the good.

-Goodness is as imaginary as happiness. Look around you, you clown.

-When we choose to view only one side of life, we can't excuse ourselves for what we then become.

-I need no excuses.

-Yet you offer them.

-Only to deflect the draining tedium of your conversation. Does the wise man quote Socrates to the monkey?

-Insults are by nature defensive. The truth must hurt. So you pull down the blinds.

-Being a self-contained creature, nothing can hurt me anymore. No longer valuing life, I don't have to be bothered by it. So it stands to reason that I don't need any defences. Go away and take your half-baked philosophy with you. You're only a common postman with delusions of grandeur. But bear in mind the unpleasant fact that you have never risen above the lowest rung of the ladder. You're a worthless plebeian. A peasant. The scum of society. We both flounder in the same drowning pool of humiliation. The difference being that I don't pretend otherwise.

-I may be a common postman, but no shame in that. I have pride. And the world at my feet.

-You have the pavements at your feet. No more.

Though neurotic, he may be right. Yet I refuse to accept this. In a complex world, a little confidence keeps at bay the threatening demons. Which are always prepared to pounce. To destroy the peace of innocent souls.

Not that my soul is innocent. Though it has been disturbed of late. Particularly during long troubled nights when I jerk awake sweating. And coughing badly. Feeling terror and despair without comprehending why. And imagining an open grave at the foot of my bed. A true horror. Even when sober.

-Mister Wernher, good-day to you.

-*Auf Wiedersehen.*

Depart with relief from this bizarre personification of broken faith. Placing the boots lightly on slow-warming stone slabs. Stopping once more to greet the twins Daniel and David. Both about to go to work. Both being mechanics. In a garage for foreign cars. Both sharing the same sports car as they share other things. Such as food, drink and girls. The charming young sods slick in slacks and suede jackets. Hush-puppies on the feet. Fair hair ruffled slightly in a light breeze. Both grinning sardonically.

-Hi, Postie!

-Daniel. David. Good-day to you.

-How's the sex life, Postie?

-A scorched wasteland, I fear.

-Sing a song of sixpence, Postie. Who are you trying to kid? Tina Louise has recently been turning her nose up at us. Instead of teasing with the tits as she usually does. It makes us suspect that someone else has been in there. And who else could it be but the sly old postman? With his silver tongue and prehistoric charm. Confess, Postie! You met her one midnight. Down a dark entry with a hard-on and a packet of rubbers.

-The entries belong to cats in heat. Not to this particular gentleman. Lads, you wrong me. Believe me.

-Man, you fracture us.

-I don't. But this electricity bill will.

-Thanks for nothing, pal.

Into their sports car and off with a roar. Waking the dozing street. Which a few seconds later reverts to dead silence. As if the world has ended. Thus making me feel unnatural. Dropping the twins' electric bill into the mailbox. And then walking on.

Around this small dog snarling happily on the pavement. Sharpening its young molars on a piece of filthy bone. Probably preparing for that day in the not-so-distant future. When it will sink those same molars into some unfortunate soul. Almost certainly me.

Such being life. According to Hans Wernher. Whom I try to forget on the approach to Pete Whelan. A man even older than I am. Also more precariously situated. Coughing, as I do, but bringing up blood as well. Which places him nearer to that abyss from which we all shy away.

-The postman!

-Morning, Pete.

-Morning.

Greets me as usual from his chair out on the pavement. With the lines of good humour in abundance around the eyes. Which have seen much of life, but have not become indifferent. Ailing body, but young at heart. Where I am healthy, but old in spirit. Or was until a few days ago. When the bad coughing started. And now aching all over. As well as in my heart. Only grateful that so far the coughing has not brought up blood. Which in truth I would rather not give away. Except at the blood-bank.

Pete is going to die.

And the mind reels instantly. From the weight of the words imagined. Causing a surge of fear that makes the heart race. And filling one with the urge to reach out and touch him. A decent urge that is resisted in a most shameful manner. Thoughts of latent homosexuality colouring good intentions with doubt. This being the sad result of too much reading about such matters. In respectable Sunday supplements and disreputable sex mags. Which inform us that male friendship is basically sexual. Though I refuse to believe it. As I smile at old Pete. With the warmth of long friendship and the pity I hope to hide. Because of the blood that stains the white of his immaculate handkerchiefs.

-And how is the wife, Pete?

-Not too good, mate. Not very well at all. Feelin' the pinch of old age. Lumbago and arthritis with side-effects from the drugs. But takes care of me as usual and rarely complains. I backed Spy Net on Saturday and won a few bob. So thought I might sneak into the West End today to buy her something small but nice from Harrods. It's not much, but it's something.

-A generous notion, Pete. And it's certainly good to see that some men still appreciate their women. Far too much selfishness and exploitation about. Not one for the male chauvinism myself.

-Well, you know, she's some woman. Always was and always will be. I only regret that the kids now live away, making her pine for them. I do my best, Postie, but she misses them. And unfortunately I'm not quite enough to make up for their loss.

-We lose what we gain. Time after time. We love our kids, and then they turn around and leave us.

-When will I win the bloody pools, mate? I'll hang on to my dentures until something comes up and I make good a few of my rash promises. Mistakes, mistakes. See, I never tried to make something special out of myself. Just lived for the day. For the moment. Never thinking that tomorrow had to come. Now it's finally here and it hurts. Since tomorrow is today and I'm nowhere.

-You're being unfair to yourself. A man does what he can. The future can rarely be predicted, so stop blaming yourself.

-Oh, aye, beware the self-pity.

-Which sneaks up upon us.

-Sit back and accept.

-That's the ticket.

Leave him sitting there. In his chair in the sunlight. Now feeling slightly fitter as I traverse these pavements. Walking out of this street. And turning into the next one. Where the living remember the virtues of the dead. And where the dying are many. And where the dogs bark in the presence of good-hearted postmen. Who drop a few letters here, a few pleasantries there. With perhaps a cup of tea. Most generously offered. To this gent who bridges the cosmic spaces between these quiet houses.

Sun becoming stronger. Sweat starting to trickle. Pains darting up the legs and the head feeling light. Was once as fit as a fiddle but lately tend to sink. Unexpectedly. As if the system is at last in revolt. With a worsening cough for good measure. Which surely means that we've caught a touch of the old bronchitis. Now a week old and growing worse with each passing day.

Though still not coughing blood. And would die with shock if I did. Lord, no, I will not go down that way. Not if *I* have my way.

Lewd fantasies again. Filling this foul mind. Thoughts of drifting along streams of velvet motion. Female lips moistly taking in the swelling flesh. While the peace of eternity silkily descends. Falling over the thoughts when I should be concentrating. On the job at hand. But instead persist in dreaming. Of loving hands tenderly at work on this burning body.

Time passing in a dream. Insubstantial forms criss-crossing the vision. Unreal. Like ghosts. The sound of traffic as a noise from distant planets. Out there in starry space. Floating forever as I once saw in a newsreel. Of an astronaut drifting in the awesome stratosphere. Far above Earth in a light-flecked black void. And experienced a chill. As if suddenly seeing Man as an ant in a boundless desert. Running in circles without known purpose or meaning. Thus left the cinema feeling like a very frightened insect. With the growing conviction that I stood at the tail-end. Of an ancient and anachronistic line. Trying to make hay while the sun shines on the edge of extinction.

Now haunted by the possibility that I might not have recovered. From that cinematic experience. Gasping for breath as I am. And contemplating a lunchtime beer. Perhaps because I'm starting to fill up with guilt. Over Eleanor Rigby's outburst and my own lack of response. Since she should have been helped. With another knock on the door. Though the ant cannot act. In a vacuum.

Hurry into this lively pub. Plant the arse on a bar-stool. Smile at the tits and ask the eyes for a pint. And a sausage. With sauce, of course. Which being cheap is all the more nourishing and aids the awareness. Of the barmaid. Who is staring strangely at me. As if seeing a ghost. Which I certainly am not. And could easily prove the point. By slapping her face and then ripping off her knickers. And ramming it up her so hard she would soon know I'm real.

-Here, Postie. Your pint.

-So kind, my dear.

How crude my suspicions. More so when I see the change. In her face which now glows with the fleeting light of compassion. If that's what it really is and I'm sure that it is. Which is why I feel frightened and want to wreak my vengeance upon her. By doing what I thought of doing a few seconds ago. Though I know that I won't do it. Because this beer is much too tasty. And because, although I fear her feminine compassion, I fear even more what might have caused it.

Yet feel the rise of violence. Uncontrollable in the breast. A great turbulence that makes my heart race and turns my face crimson.

Good bit of sausage. A nice drop of beer. Cooling the palate. And the fever.

Chapter Ten

-Well, lookahere! It's the silver-tongued postman again!

-A rare treat t' be sure. At this time of the day dat is.

-Mister Brown. Mister Murphy. How are you?

-Recovered, ready to go, and otherwise normal. The *normal* part being more than we can say for you.

-It bein' that ya never drink at lunchtime. Sure what would be the special occasion, Postie?

-Marge, a pint, please. And one each for my two thirsty friends.

-He's gone insane at last!

-That he has. But at least it's made him generous.

-Gentlemen, a toast. To old age and the coming of infirmity.

-I'll drink to that.

-I'll drink t' anyt'ing.

-And now, Marge, another. When you're ready. Also for these good friends.

-Guzzling. That's what a man likes.

-A thousand blessings on deranged postmen.

-Gentlemen, I'll drink to that.

-I'll drink t' anyt'ing.

-Aren't you feeling well, Postie?

-I am not.

-The dogs bite in darkest night.

-They do.

-Postie, you look pale.

-Mister Brown, I *feel* pale.

-Another pint is what ya need.

-Very true, Mister Murphy. Hardly noticed the time passing. Marge, three more. And whatever you would like for yourself. Spare no expense.

-You should go home, Postie. You look unwell.

-Woman's sympathy is a godsend. Now the beers. If you will.

-Dat's what I like. The foam on top. Like a milkshake wit'out the fuckin' straw.

-Belt it into you, Irish.

–Dat I will. In tribute to our Postman, here.

-Who graciously accepts the tribute.

-Postie, I worry about you. This extravagance.

-This old heart is boundless.

-Dat it is. An' I'm almost halfway through this pint and t'inkin' of the next.

-Forthcoming. Marge!

-Hey, hold *on* a minute!

-Now don't ya be stoppin' him now, Archie. Life's short enough as it is, so let's drink while we can. Never know when the well will run dry.

-Gentlemen, this brow is feverish. This tongue remains parched. I need the amber refreshment.

-It's unbelievable!

-It's the end of the fuckin' world. Goin' out wit' a bang.

-Mister Murphy, I believe you may be right. Marge, three more, please.

-Postie, have you stopped work for the day?

-I have not.

-Don't you believe it!

-When I look into the bottom of this glass I see the wee leprechauns. Dancin' about in pixie hats. And playin' their flutes. Like the patriotic Irishmen they are.

-Gentlemen, to the leprechauns.

-I'll drink to that.

W.A. Harbinson

-I'll drink t' anyt'ing.

-Mister Brown. Mister Murphy. A man comes to the September of his years and looks back to see that the long travails have led nowhere.

-What?

-Say dat again.

-Friends, Romans and Countrymen, I am no longer at peace. The old ticker hammers like a gong. And lewd fantasies flicker through a demented brain.

-It's poetry. Dat's what it is. Pure poetry and horse-shite.

-Maybe you *do* need another beer, Postie.

-Dear Marge. Please kindly refill these opaque goblets.

-Are you talking about the beer glasses?

-I am.

-Gee, how cute!

-Postie, you've won a heart.

-Wit' a nice piece of rump.

-Mister Murphy, you're uncouth.

-Dat I am.

-Gentlemen, to the struggling Catholic Irish.

-I'll drink to that.

-I'll drink t' anyt'ing.

-Old friends, stout companions, we relax with a very nice drop this day.

-Do you mean the beer or the barmaid?

-A good question, dat.

-Gentlemen, we relax with *two* nice drops today.

-A toast.

-T' drops.

-And drips.

-Would ya be suggestin' a disease I never had?

-Gentlemen, gentlemen. Social diseases this conversation can do without.

-Agreed.

-And seconded. Here's t' benevolent postmen.

–A worthy toast.

-Can't do it, Postie.

-Why not?

-Empty glass.

-Marge. Three more. With straws.

-This morning a drunkard. This afternoon a good Samaritan. Must have been struck by a bolt of bloody lightning.

-Lightning alone. There was no blood on it.

-Smart sod.

-Here's t' the smart sods that buy us the liquid lunch.

-I'll drink to that.

-I'll drink t' anyt'ing.

-In the September of a man's years he takes to drink and once more sees the sunlight.

-What?

-Say dat again.

-Friends, Romans and Countrymen, I begin to feel at peace again. And sprightly. Springs in the shoes and a song in the heart.

-A good fucking feeling.

-And religious.

-Beware, comrades. I may discard this heavy mailbag and hurl myself bodily upon yonder barmaid.

-Won't beware.

-Be watchful.

-And so learn many things.

-Does the baby teach its fat-er t' walk?

-Mister Murphy, you lack humility.

-Never havin' heard of the word I'd have t' agree wit' ya.

-Mister Brown, what do you think of Miss Eleanor Rigby?

-I don't.

-She's in love with you.

-Is that a fact?

-It is.

-I don't believe a word of it.

-Gentlemen, here's to Miss Eleanor Rigby.

-I'll drink to that.

-I'll drink t' anyt'ing.

-My, how the time flies. Marge, kindly replenish these empty glasses.

-Postie, are you going to carry that bag or sleep in it? I mean, after lunch.

-Business as usual. Just as in show-business, I never fail to show. And am countless times warmly blessed for it.

-A noble creature. One that works for a livin'.

-Mister Brown, you should be out looking for a job today. Please recall what the milkman said. No money, no milk.

-I'll start looking tomorrow. When your benevolent lunacy has passed.

-Sure kindness is a wonderful t'ing. Even if it only comes in small doses.

-I'll drink to that.

-I'll drink t' anyt'ing.

-Gentlemen, what happened to the counter? My elbow is unable to locate it.

-Beware the pull of gravity.

-Which doesn't stop the rise of other t'ings.

-Uncouth, Mister Murphy. Uncultured.

-But a fine heritage. Steeped in t' past.

-Where it should bloody-well stay.

-Dat's an insult.

-That's a fact.

-Gentlemen, peace.

-Shake, ya bastard.

-Done.

-I feel light, good comrades. Of mind and body. Like Fred Astaire with his top hat. And a cane. Very much appreciate it if I could dance upon that table.

-Watch it, Postie!

-Sure you'll break your bloody neck!

-Timber!

-Gentlemen, your assistance. If you would be so kind. I don't believe I can move this broken back.

-Sure dat was a great height ya fell from.

-Too true.

-A successful venture, gentlemen. Had it not been for the poor craftsmanship employed in the construction of that table. Furniture is not what it used to be.

-Postie, you're normally very nice and I don't like to say this, but you're going to have to pay to have that table repaired.

-Have no fear, Marge. Just present me with the bill upon completion of the task. Now three more pints. If you will.

-What tits!

-T' be warmed against.

-Nature's own jewels.

-The Postie here is a rare wit.

-Who gives us free beers in his moment of madness.

-The Postie is nothing but a spluttering spark of life. Briefly aglow in eternal night. And crying out in protest.

-What?

-Say dat again.

-Friends, Romans and Countrymen, I am not as young as I once was. So here's a toast to Fred Astaire, who stays young for all of us.

-I'll drink to that.

-I'll drink t' anyt'ing.

-Mister Murphy, be honest now. Define Ireland.

-A bogland swamped in self-servin' myths.

-Mister Brown, define England.

-A sick soul sunk by its stinking snobbery.

-Mister Postman, define the postman.

-A carrier of dreams borne of failure.

-The man that buys me a beer isn't a failure.

-Until he stops buyin'.

-I must think about dat.

-Marge, three more pints. With the foam on top. And the straws.

-Fantastic!

-If the world must end, let it end in a flood.

-Gentlemen, I feel sad. Here I stand, with companions stout and true, feeling human again. But soon I must be off about my duties, serving the Queen and her country. To which we all owe so much. So. I should not be standing here in idle dalliance. But should be back in the Post Office, preparing for the afternoon's deliveries. Whilst taking the abuse of a self-castrated eunuch. Who is deemed to be my superior and behaves accordingly. Dear God, the injustice of life cripples me.

-Down that beer and deaden the pain.

-Sure it's t' only way.

-Comrades, I should never have married.

-There's a fact!

-Were it not for my heavy responsibilities, I would join you in the ranks of the philosophically sound unemployed.

-That ya should. And be a better man for it.

-A fucking disaster. If the Postie doesn't do an honest day's work, who's to pay for the pints?

-I must t'ink about dat.

-Gentlemen, a slight nausea arises.

-At what?

-Not *at* what. *In* what?

-My stomach.

-To the toilet, Postie.

-In what direction?

-We've turned you around. Now just follow your nose.

-I shall never make it.

-You want one of my pockets?

-That grease-proofed bag should suffice for now.

-That's good. Sausage in, sausage out. Now minced when once it was solid. Meet Mister Postman, the walking liquidiser.

-Hide the bag, gentlemen. For the sake of the remaining

dignity. Lest someone observe my shame.

-Who owns this mohair coat on the hanger?

-The businessman seated in yonder corner.

-He won't know it's in his pocket until he leaves.

-Would ya be feelin' any better, Postie?

-A great relief, I assure you.

-An awful stench around here, Postie. Dead giveaway. Better smother it in three more beers.

-An excellent notion. Marge, if you will.

-Hey, boys, who spewed?

-That businessman seated in yonder corner.

-Filthy bastard. Now three more beers for the gentlemen.

-Friends, Romans and Countrymen, I drink this beer only as a curative. Here's to my everlasting good health.

-I'll drink to that.

-I'll drink t' anyt'ing.

-The time has come, the Walrus said.

-Postie is leaving us?

-In our hour of need?

-He is. Gentlemen, the truth. Am I?

-What?

-Drunk again?

-Yesh.

-Then I must be off.

-Okay.

-Adios.

-Peace, brothers.

Chapter Eleven

Pissed as a newt. Drunk as a skunk. Tralala-dadee. Humming sweet melodies with sour breath. As we skip rather friskily up and down the pavement. Where passers-by stop and stare. Outraged by such behaviour. Especially from a public servant. On duty with the heavy bag thumping his aching ribs. As he performs his little Fred Astaire spoof. Beads of sweat on his forehead but not giving a damn. Not even for the dry, spasmodic coughing that interrupts his slurred song.

Afternoon, sir, and tip the peaked cap. Afternoon, madam, and lecherously leer. Nothing to lose but an almost worthless job. And a certain amount of pride. Booze for lunch and guilt, no doubt, for supper.

Back at the Post Office Miss Emily Forthright was aghast. Saying good heavens Postie you're drunk. With consternation written all over her darling face. As well as a touch of pity. Wondering what misfortune had befallen the postman. Driving him to brazenly obvious lunchtime drinking. But called me a poor man and gave me a cup of tea. Steaming hot and thickly sugared for the sobriety promised therein. Trying to repair the damage before the return of Mister Fish. Our hot-arsed superior. Though was really quite surprised when I pressed my hand to her belly. Saying if hell's below I'll try it right now. Yet still she gave me a friendly smile. Perhaps even coquettish. Intrigued by the good-natured daring of this wicked old fool.

-Tralala-dadee!

This afternoon of seemingly endless gloomy streets.

Pavements shifting suspiciously underfoot. Though I do feel athletic. This clearly being a sign that drunkenness doth prevail. Poor weak mortal that I am. If not failing to notice. That lately I tend to fall to pieces far too quickly. To find my thoughts swimming with phantoms and portends of doom.

Always suspected the ageing process, but this is ridiculous. And made even more so by this sickening cough. A touch of the old bronchitis that has lingered long under the surface.

-Tralala-dadee!

Humming songs smiling. And dwelling on lewd thoughts more frequently than ever. Seeing bouncing breasts and welcoming thighs whilst hearing arousing erotic words. And almost palpably feeling the moist softness of searching lips. Which could ease the pain of more cruel recollections. As the ticker unfortunately races faster than before. Beating like a bell tolling the mortal hours away. With a trembling of the limbs that is caused by rising fear. Darkening the sexual fantasies that once were enjoyable. Such being the nature of the depravity that has lately come upon me. A product of the evil that lurks deep within. Those trying to break free from the body and take wing in the ether.

-Tralala-dadee!

The streets through which I pass are like corridors in a bad dream. One I recall from as far back as the womb. As if, indeed, I am heading right back there. To curl up in mindless peace and sheltering darkness. Singing tralala-dadee. But unable to get past that. With nausea bubbling up and the mind in growing chaos. Temporarily. One hopes. As one could not for long tolerate these uneasy thoughts. Thus tonight a few more beers. With which to calm the deepening fevers. And to hell with the consequences. Which will come from the wife. Who will have to be informed that an alligator chased me. Right into the house of that helpful Mister Brown. Who doesn't think of Miss Rigby though she yearns daily for him. With all the romantic passion of an innocent spinster. Her dreams being the kind we have all known.

Though now prefer to forget.

-Tralala-dadee.

Now singularly aware that many eyes are fixed upon me. Staring at me as if at an alien being. From outer space where such creatures might exist. With multiple heads and prismatic eyes. Dreadful sights to behold. Even worse than those rendered vividly in one's bad dreams. But remarkably intelligent and sardonically amused. By our illogical social habits. And quaint religious beliefs. As they academically study Earth. That wee piece of dirt they found floating in space. Thinking how interesting are these self-defeating Earthlings. Building only to destroy. Eating only to shit. Drinking only to piss. Surrendering all pride for a lunacy known as love. Fumbling and stumbling. At the tail-end of a grotesque biological experiment. Dreaming of the infinite while trapped in their finite flesh. As this postman is right now. And in truth always was. Every noble aspiration curtailed by more immediate needs. Such as boozing and fucking. And the thought of tomorrow's breakfast. Though it being that food merely goes in one end. To come out the other. One sees no sense at all in the process.

So praise be to God. For His divine incompetence. Which is not for we mere mortals to question.

-Trala. Lala. Dadee...

Ach, these old bones ache. While the skin crawls uncomfortably. Yet I cannot break loose from the useless dead weight of my mortal armour. Might be true, after all, that life is cursed even before it begins. That we are born as gods and die as whimpering things.

Yes? No! What am I thinking? I refuse to accept this sick man's ephemeral nightmare. It will pass. Please God, let it pass. It will surely pass...

Trala... Lee... Deeda...

Once more this street of dreams. And without thinking filthy. Knock, knock. On the door of the delirious Miss Rigby. This time prepared. To offer words of advice. Without foolish reserve. Eye to eye with the honesty of extreme inebriation. So knock, knock. And receive no response.

God bless that fragile soul. With her secret dreams and torments. For either she is still drunk or too ashamed to come out. Not knowing that mockery is not my intention. Only sympathy and understanding. And perhaps a sly glance to ascertain if that brassiere-strap is really necessary. For the support of hitherto fore unsuspected mammary treasures.

More to Miss Rigby than meets the eye. Which is something I've always known. As I've also always known that her body was rather good. If sadly unused. Though not without the latent lasciviousness. The very thought of which warms this postman's vibrant loins. And makes his treasured manhood stand upright in salute. As he stoops down to whisper salutations through this brass mailbox.

-I desire you, Miss Rigby. I *want* you. Please come out and reveal yourself.

While automatically sniffing to check that there's no suicidal gas. Not for one minute considering that the neighbours might be watching. And calling the police with information about sexual deviants. Who play Peeping Tom. With unprotected spinsters. Who do not as a rule reply to voices whispering through their mailboxes. But instead merely respond with a mice-like scuffling within. Thus advertising the fact that life at least continues. And is able to make us blush. At the knowledge of her demented confession and subsequent shame. Which doubtless she is feeling this very moment.

-How dare you!

Sweet suffering shit. That terrible sound. Making me jerk away from the mailbox flushing with guilt. Spinning around with a groan of horror. At the sight of Missus Whittaker who is pink-faced and glaring. And spitting into my right eye. The one that was straining to see into Miss Rigby's hallway. With only the best of intentions.

Oh me. Oh my. Better straighten the tie. Then also

straighten the shoulders as we face her. Feign unruffled calm.

-My dear good lady.

-Don't you dear-good-lady me! You filthy old goat! I always 'ad me doubts about you and now they're confirmed. Disgustin' Peepin' Tom that you are, you sexual detergent -

-Degenerate.

-And general scum-bag. Caught in the very act! Spyin' through a single woman's mailbox and clearly pantin' with lust. God Almighty! And to think I've got two little girls of my own, both runnin' around without protection. I'm takin' a chance just lettin' 'em play in the streets, but what else can a poor mother do?

-Please, Madam. Kindly control your unseemly hysteria.

-And stinkin' of drink while supposedly still on duty. Eyes red as two coals in a hot grate. I'll report you for sure this time. No two ways about it. Drunkenness and perversion while deliverin' the Queen's mail. Whisperin' obscenities through mailboxes, peepin' through keyholes –

-It was not the keyhole.

– and attackin' innocent childern. To all this I have witnesses.

-What witnesses?

-My poor helpless girls.

-Filthy liars, the pair of them.

-Disparchment of character as well. I'll add that to the charges.

-The word is *disparagement*.

-That's it. Along with lechery, drunkenness and violence against the innocent under-aged. Twenty years if you get a bloody day. I'll personally see to it.

Impertinent bitch. Ought to knock her ugly head off her shoulders. And would, too. Were it not for the size of her. Since one blow from her and I'd be bedridden for a month. Though still cannot tolerate such venom from the hag. Patience and pride have their limits and mine have been reached. Not one for letting the drink talk but will take no more nonsense. And refuse to let the cow disconcert me. It being that I do not pay for the privilege of this job. By letting slatterns be free with their wild accusations. No, certainly not. Always good, myself, for the innovative repartee. The highly relevant come-back. So to hell with the Senior Postmaster, the pay-packet, the wife. Here goes nothing with this richly textured mouthful.

-My dear good lady. Forgive the indiscretion. But were it not for the gentlemanly inbred couth and culture, I would happily slap you senseless for those rude remarks. Indeed, never in all of my twenty years of service have I suffered such unfounded accusations. I would therefore remind you, Madam, that you only pay rent for that pig-stye four doors farther along, not for the whole street. So kindly take your disgusting presence back to your own trough. And, if you have any more to say, please say it from there.

-Don't you threaten *me* with them fancy airs and graces. I know your type. Think you're the ant's pants because you wear a uniform, but you're nothin' but a common wanker in disguise.

-Uniform of the Queen, Madam. Please don't forget that. And it's a uniform that you're thieving bookie husband could not hope to wear.

-That's it! Insultin' my 'usband! Now you're for it, you shit!

-The fact that he's married to you is surely insult enough. No need for me to add to it. So I just speak the facts.

-Cheeky bastard! You cunt!

And lets fly with her open hand. Which is large as well as unwashed. Which I notice as I duck. And swish! Goes the hand. Through molecular space. While she follows it forward impelled by her own momentum. And twists sideways into the gutter where she seems right at home. If temporarily bewildered. Cursing me with conviction as I change my own direction. To cut obliquely across the road to the house of Hans Wernher. That extremely bitter hunchback with delusions of grandeur. Now seated on his doorstep. And grinning maliciously at me. As behind me the Great Bitch bawls more abuse. Obscene threats for the whole street to hear. Thus making me even more aware. Of what I'm holding in my free hand. Namely, a plain brown envelope. Containing pornographic pix. All the way from the infamous Boogie Street in naughty Singapore. To land hotly in this celibate's cold lap.

-Mister Wernher, good day.

-Postie, I confess. Some times I almost feel proud of you. You're an inveterate snob. Which means you still manage to discriminate. It would appear that Missus Whittaker is after your hide. A sure sign that you can't be *totally* worthless.

-Mister Wernher, I have a small package for you.

-Take note, I will throw it into the loo.

Hand him the bulging envelope. Which he flips carelessly over his shoulder. To let it rest as usual on the hallway floor. With all his other unopened mail. This being something that we forgot to take into consideration. Thus possibly wasting a quid and much feverish anxiety. And losing the sort of victory that one could truly cherish. More so since one's career might be drawing to a close. The cough, the light head and the feeling of impending lunacy all combining to offend the Almighty. So continue to talk. As pleasantly as possible. Until we can persuade him to open the envelope. Thus opening the door to sleepless nights of sexual derangement.

-Mister Wernher. Will you never read your mail?

-That bulky envelope looked different. Obviously not from my idiot-parents. So maybe I'll open it later.

-That's nice to know.

- Postie, are you ill? You certainly look it.

-I'm drunk.

-An excellent condition. Weakens the body while releasing the mind. At the moment, like those amphibians of old, we cannot take too much of this rarefied air. But the evolutionary process decrees that eventually we must do so. Man is slowly evolving from matter into pure mind. And alcohol, as well as sex

133

or certain drugs, offers us a glimpse into our full potential. Which is why we're a nation of drunks, dope-addicts and sex-fiends.

-You're way beyond me already.

-Perhaps. Listen, Postie. I've never offered a confession before, but I have one to offer to you now. If my insults have been more cutting with you than with others, it's because of my suspicion that I might have a certain amount of respect for you. You're a rogue draped in a cloak of theatrical civility, but I believe that you're only trying to disguise decency and a generous heart. Yet lately you've been a changed man. One trying to hide his fears. Indeed, you seem to be at the end of your tether. *Are* you in such a state?

-If I was, I would hardly know about it.

-Or hardly acknowledge it. Good afternoon, Postie.

Slam. Goes the door. Right in my face. Something that seems to be happening with increasing regularity. Though one must admit. That that *was* a rare conversation. Between me and the Kraut. Some of it beyond me. But some of it echoing thoughts that have recently chilled me. Since I did not for one moment appreciate that particular comment. About the possibility of my being at the end of my tether.

Far from it, in fact. Spread the news throughout the land. A man simply grows more mellow. In the September of his years. Brooding a little more about his all too finite future. And his degenerating body. Thus leading his mind to seek some fresh form of stimulation. And yet. Come to think of it. Regarding such I was always the same.

May be a common postman, but always had uncommon ways. Learned a lot from my large dictionary and could always put a word or two together. Never lacked regard for learning. And always encouraged it in others. Such as my son, Ross. Who often clutters up the living-room. Experimenting with electric-wiring and currents carried magically in the atmosphere. These days bounced off satellites. Or so he has informed me. So must ask him more about it. Some fine day in the distant future. It being a mysterious and most fascinating subject. Making me rather proud that I never believed in Heaven. Nor in angels with wings strumming harps under haloes. Though now surprised that Hans Wernher believes in me in his odd, bitter way.

The comforting glow of booze beginning to leave this haunted mind. Which might indeed be at the end of its tether. Opening its gates to another flood of nausea and dread.

A bad state of affairs. When mere alcohol has this effect. On a man with a taste for it. Though. Come to think of it. The cough hasn't helped any. And. Between the stares of old friends and the comments of hunchbacks. A man starts to feel worse than he might actually be. Particularly when even the barmaid looked thoughtfully at me. Then whispered what were clearly concerned words to other customers. Thus causing me to feel an unreasonable anger. Something to which I was once rarely prone. Having always believed that wasted emotion is a singular vice.

Have to admit, nonetheless. To great changes within. Doubtless quite natural and encouraged by this bad cough. And a pox on the recurrent bronchitis. Which will have me yet. As it is having me this very moment before this young lady.

-Hi, Postie.

How sexy she looks. This sixteen-year-old. Standing before me in blue denims and a sweater. Everything tight against her shapely young body. Thus revealing the curves of thrusting breasts and flat belly. As I rise in my own heat. And dissolve into my loins. Feeling lust and shame at once. It being that she is younger than my own sexy daughter. One fact I cannot avoid thinking about. Even as I lose control. Manhood springing to life. Poking at underpants stretched more taut than usual. With more vigour than is customary for someone my age. Thus managing to convince me that I should see a doctor. For an accurate diagnosis. Before being punctured by needles and sinking down sighing. Under heavy sedation. Clearly needed as I smile at this enticing Lolita. Flashing good teeth and pretending that all is perfectly normal.

-Miss Bleakley, you surprise me. But pleasantly so. Delighted to see you, as usual, sucking your thumb in the doorway.

-Gee, Postie, do you always talk like that?

-Since before I could walk.

-I wish I knew some *younger* guys who could talk like you. I always seem to meet the deadbeats. Or maybe they're *all* like that nowadays.

-Come, come, my pet. Such gloomy thoughts are not appropriate to the likes of you. I would rather see amusement in those lovely eyes. Not this premature cynicism.

-Amusement. Some joke. If you knew what I'm having to endure, you'd go cut your throat. It's real hell, I'm telling you.

-At sweet sixteen?

-You better believe it.

-I'm sorry. I can't.

-Christ, just look around you. Isn't this place a drag during the day? Dead as a doornail. Not a soul about. Unemployed, I'm beginning to feel that I'm embalmed. Come inside, Postie, and have a cup of tea. Talk to me before I start climbing the walls.

-Delighted, my dear.

Would normally have refused, but this time don't have the strength. A cup of tea. With perhaps a sandwich. Might help to ease the sickness. Since certainly no licentious activities are intended. As I enter this gloomy house. Though doubt that I'd refuse. If she offered it on a plate. Instead of a sandwich. Being unable to think in my present condition. Of anything more alluring than young, willing flesh. Inciting me to imagine. Thighs parting smooth belly sweat-slicked heaving breasts. Mouth open moist lips pouting teasingly. All of which makes me quiver. Like a plucked banjo-string. Thinking of my coarse bulk upon her fragile frame. Humping and heaving pushing tight to one another. Joined at the hip, legs and arms intertwined. Pushing harder and deeper running short of breath and sense.

Which I lack at the moment as she closes the door behind her. And stares at me where I stand in silence in this dimly-lit interior.

-Take a chair, Postie.

-Thank you.

Obeying the sweet young thing. Sitting down and glancing around this small room in this working-class house. Spick and span and rather sterile. Not a book in sight. Her parents being tidy folk. With tidy, untutored minds. Thus making me feel starved already. For want of intellectual stimulation. Which we could do with ourselves. Being hypocritically critical. As we place the canvas mailbag by the booted feet on the carpet. Sinking into this cosy armchair. With its mass-produced hand-printed covering. As gaudily coloured as fresh vomit. Though I still bless the parents. For kindly going out to work. Thus enabling me to watch their sexy daughter in the kitchen. Where she chatters about nothing in weary maturity. Before coming back out to place a tray on the coffee-table. Teapot-spout steaming quite splendidly right there in front of me.

-Your tea, Postie. And I thought you might need a sandwich.

-Why?

-'Cause you look awful.

-Thank you.

She smiles. Lowering herself into the chair directly facing me. Legs crossed in the blue denims tight on firm thighs. Displaying delicate ankles and small feet in rubber flip-flops. Toes curled as I imagine they would also curl in sex. When tickling my marbles. Thus encouraging an erection. Of the kind that I have not had in a fairly long time. Which is a thought to cast aside. As we both sit here sipping and nibbling. So instead must keep talking. Until the sandwiches run out. At which point I might be offered more. Than mere bread and tea.

-Miss Louise, you're not working today.

-No. I got bounced. They said I couldn't keep my mind on

137

what I was doing. Which was certainly true. Not that I mind much. Since I've got other things to think about.

-Such as?

-Ah, *you* know. *All* sorts of things.

-Ah, yes. I see.

-Jesus, Postie, you've got a really nice smile. Are those teeth your own?

-I appreciate that particular enquiry. And, yes, they're my own.

-Gee, how did you manage that, Postie? I mean, at your age and all.

-I brush them three times a time. With the blood of innocent virgins. From whom I steal when the full moon is on view. Vampire tendencies, you know.

-Aw, come *on*, Postie!

-Believe me or believe me not. But tell me: how's the love-life?

-Don't ask.

-And the boyfriend?

-Oh, him… The creep's worried.

-About what?

-Pregnant girlfriends. Of which I am one. And at sweet sixteen. Shit.

Deary me, how embarrassing. Not used to such confessions from sublime teenage beauties. Particularly when they stare at me with spoon-sized, moist eyes. As she is doing right now. Doubtless waiting for me to utter outraged words of condemnation. Which I am not about to do. Being too mature and understanding. And also surprisingly short on words.

-Did you hear me, Postie?

-Yes.

-Well?

-Well what?

-Listen, Postie. I'm telling you this because you're the only person I know who might listen without biting my head off. Now

138

what do I *do*? I mean, I haven't even told my parents yet. You know what *they're* like. Don't drink or smoke, go to church every Sunday, and always boasting about what a good girl I am. Except I'm *not* a good girl. I'm just a girl and I generally like what I am. Or did until this came up. And now I'm not at all sure. God, I wouldn't mind being pregnant if it was only me involved. But it's not. It's also *them*. It's my parents and my friends and what they'll all say. I mean, nobody – at least no one that *I* can think of – is going to understand or forgive. Will they, Postie? Now, *will they*?

Then the tears. Which I sensed were coming. Dribbling gleaming down the flushed cheeks. Closed eyes weeping on crossed arms. Until her bowed head hides her face. Her body, so shapely, now shaking as if in a fever.

Which leaves only two choices. To the mortified postman. Either crawl into his mailbag to hide like a mouse or sneak out of the house like a rat. A third alternative, of course, is to try talking to her. Though in truth this does not hold too great an appeal. Cowardice being something of an intimate acquaintance. Not helping while I think to offer something more constructive. But alas cannot do so. Since I would then be compelled to say that her parents will understand. When we both know they won't. Or, not saying that, would have to say that it doesn't matter. When we both know it does. And meanwhile, while the Postie procrastinates, her sobbing continues.

God, what can one do? To melt the ice of this frozen tongue. Which knowing not how to release itself lies forlorn in the mouth. Yet really must say something. No matter how inadequate. So lean forward in this chair and clear the throat. Hoping to sound calm and wise.

-The young man. What does he say about this?

-He'll marry me.

-Do you want that?

-Is there a choice?

-A hard one. But a choice.

-I'll marry him, thanks. After all, Postie, he actually *wants* to marry me. Guys are *like* that at eighteen, the poor sods, thinking sex is a miracle. But Jesus, oh God, don't you *understand*, Postie? It's not him. It's not *me*. It's not the baby. *It's what they'll all say*!

Sobbing violently again. Her body twisting away in shame. A black line of mascara smeared down one burning cheek. Her fingers outspread on her face, hoping to hide the reality.

Which I, also, cannot bear. Knowing it to be true and therefore unavoidable. Namely, what they will say. Neither me nor even God being able to prevent it. Such being the way of the old-fashioned world to which her religious parents cling grimly.

Defeated, the postman stands up. Weighed down by his helplessness. To heft the canvas bag onto his shoulder. Stung by the knowledge that failure, no matter how accidental, seems to predominate this particular afternoon. Which, mercifully, is deepening into the early evening. The dimming light of which is falling upon his scuffling booted feet. Which are attempting to make an unobtrusive, cowardly exit. And, failing, force him to speak at last into the wall of her sobbing.

-I'm sorry. I think I'd better leave.

-Yes! Yes! Please go! *Please*!

Most pathetically, disgustingly grateful for this reprieve. So even as she renews her sobbing, hurry outside. To find grey sky. Low cloud. Deep shadow. Cool air. And the fierce Missus Whittaker on her doorstep along the street. Looking on. Smirking. Forehead wrinkled over gleaming eyes. Two muscular arms crossed.

In judgement.

Chapter Twelve

Now going down. As silent as a submarine. Into depths dark and aquatically exotic. Bizarre colours and shapes. Dead faces in the weeds. Leering frozenly. The ones who sank from sight as the precious years passed. With nothing to show for them but a ribbon of dreams. Containing amber fluids and smoke-obscured figures. In this and other pubs of time immemorial. While tingtingaling! Goes the pinball machine. Above voices happily clashing. The vibrant talk ricocheting in the head and rendering it senseless.

Now here in this place of purely physical release. Legs spread and cock out pissing urgently. White tiles and concrete trough. The snot-green bile of vomit. Which was fresh from the throat not two minutes ago when the pains in the guts were so fierce.

Relieved and exultant sweeping out through the door. Reeling back through this heterosexual gay crowd to the bar. With the fist on the counter encouraging prompt service. And the barmaid saying loudly good God you look sick. The indelicate bitch. Whose business it isn't. And who might for her comment get a swift boot up the arse. Though even the mere thought of such exertion gives rise to exhaustion. And makes us yearn even more for a cooling pint of the best. To pour down this hot throat which being ravaged is rasping. While the mind also ravaged is reeling into other worlds. Making us long for oblivion. In the night's boundless darkness.

-For Jasus sake, Postie, ya should be off home. In yer bed.

141

Sure ya don't look well at all. And you're sweatin' like you've just had a long wank.

-I *am* home, Mister Murphy. So are you. Now. Here. Where we both belong.

-Sure, Postie, ya don't sound yourself. Not a bit of it. And ya look like a vampire. Bloodless. Just like me fat'er before he passed on.

-Please, Mister Murphy, not now. Marge, two more pints. If you will.

-You shouldn't.

-I shall.

This lunacy flickering like a tendril of flame. Hot as blue ice on the bared beating heart. As I see the wasted face of my good friend Mister Murphy. As wrinkled tissue paper stretched over bone and blood. While jostling all around me the other skeletons are rejoicing. Dancing on their tombstones. Under pitiless cosmic skies. Remarkably lively when they move with bones rattling. Mocking the mortality of the humans gathered along this sodden bar.

Just one more pint. And then the end will come. Causing me to slide to the floor. In a whimpering heap. Merely one more crushed insect in the jaws of evolution. To be reclaimed tomorrow morning over breakfast with the wife. As well as male and female offspring. Who will likely be accusing. Though certainly not ignored. By me until death do us part. As it must. In the end.

Shocking thoughts this evening. The interior monologue of a loonie. Which causes one to tremble with increasing trepidation. Sensing that one has finally gone beyond the pale. The senses collapsing into terminal disrepair. Thus encouraging another intake of beer. To ease the mounting pressure. Indifferent to the protests of barmaid and friends. The hours having passed quickly to cast me adrift. From everything except anger. While I try to accept. That I might suddenly be an old man. With Death the Grim Reaper whose scythe glitters in my dreams. While he in his black cloak leers chalky-faced at me. As I violently cough my way out of troubled sleep. And jerk upright sweating. And groaning most audibly. Beside the wife, the missus, who if not asleep would scold me. As she will tomorrow morning. If I do not return home this evening in a state of sobriety.

-Mister Murphy, there's a demon at my feet.

-What's dat?

-Digging a hole in the floor.

-What's dat again?

-For I feel myself sinking.

-Is dat a fact?

-Deep down. To the centre of the Earth.

-Me arm's under yer shoulder, Postie. So ya can't sink much farther.

-Bless you, Mister Murphy. All is well again.

-Ya should be home, Postie. Sure yer not a well man. I can tell dat.

-Your round, Mister Murphy.

-Two more it is, den. On the last of my unemployment money, though that wouldn't concern ya.

Enjoy staring down into amber-coloured beer. Trying to discern the reflection of my nose. Which is, at this moment, rather aglow. Meet Mister Postman, the walking traffic-light. Who burns bright with a minimum of fuel. Of an alcoholic nature. Without which he dies a little. At least lately, if never before.

Note that the coughing has diminished with drink. Thus giving reasonable grounds for this gross inebriation. Something I will need when eventually facing the wife. An experience I do not relish. Having had that menagerie right up to the neck. And. Though refusing to let the beer talk. Will brook no impertinence this evening.

No, indeed not. And never again. One slip of the tongue and we'll wreck the whole house. Windows, furniture, son and daughter, the lot. Thus releasing the resentment one has harboured for so long. Because of one's low income this past twenty-odd years. Most hocked for the quick knock one had in one's youth. In an entry strewn with rubbish and patrolled by cats in heat. She and I never again to look at each other. With the passion of that one night. Long gone and now lost forever. A penance quietly sanctioned by a sanctimonious society. The indecency of which has often threatened to drive me to the brink. And is possibly doing so this very minute.

-Mister Murphy, have one more for the road.

-Alcoholic poisonin'. If ya die of nothin' else, ya'll die of dat.

-Marge. Two more, please.

-Please, Postie. Don't.

-Your concern touches this forlorn heart. Now two more. Without further ado.

The waters swirling dangerously in the mind's turbulent reservoir. Vaporous ghosts leering from the shadows of bygone times. Haunting. Accusing. Mouthing accusations of failure. Which I take to be the product of life's lousy betrayals. For did not see much success. And certainly never expected much. Though was not prepared for this total bewilderment. And the fear that swarms like lice beneath my burning skin.

Oh me. Oh my. Should not be thinking this way. Which, being morbid, would once have been alien to me. Yet cannot resist my own colourful flights of fancy. Recalling that as a child I was thrilled by a recurrent dream. Before the dreams of the flesh. A dream of a black-armoured knight bestride a snow-white horse. Charging over green fields holding high a fluttering pennant. Until distant guns fired. Causing flame and swirling smoke. Which, disappearing, revealed the pennant tattered. And the noble knight's bare arse exposed. Such being the nature of life. Which eventually leaves all of us starkers.

-Mister Murphy, I will now leave this place.

-Ya say it like yer goin' t' the moon.

-Farther, Mister Murphy. Much farther.

-Farther than dat is a long way.

-Remove your arm from beneath my shoulder. I require no assistant.

-But yer legs do.

-They shall act for themselves.

-Now is dat a fact?

-It is.

-Postie, yer unwell.

-Mister Murphy, you repeat yourself.

-Some t'ings require repeatin'.

-The truth, Mister Murphy. Am I?

-What?

-Drunk again.

-Yesh.

-Then I must be off again.

Dimly-lit and long the streets. The corridors of a dream. Walking unsteadily but sprightly nevertheless. Feet smacking the pavements suspiciously insubstantial. Under low clouds. Which have densely gathered to block out the light. And keep it off my body which, though in its uniform, shivers. In the grip of a chill wind that also moans mournfully. As the heart goes boom-boom and bones creak like rusty hinges. Making the blood pump as people pass by in pairs. Or alone or in groups. Jostling, Elbowing. Truly too much to take. So grab hold of this passing woman. By the hair of her head. To hurl her sideways forcefully into that red-brick wall. Causing female screaming, a male oath, the onrush of a clenched fist. Which comes out of the twilight and rapidly enlarges. And then makes my head explode into showering stars and pain. A rising pool of oblivion as I sink to the pavement. Where I hear shouts and muttering from above. *He attacked her the bastard the cunt's mad give him the boot.* The latter being what the Postie secretly wants. But doesn't receive. Doubtless thanks to the women. And their naturally kind hearts. Or more likely their reluctance to be involved with the Law.

Thus. Sounds of shuffling. As male brutes are dragged away. Cursing and boasting and probably waving fists. To disappear and leave the Postie in peace here where he lies. In this gutter with bloody lips. Mumbling his defiance. And relishing his pain. Which is at least something sharp enough to keep fear at bay.

Time having passed now back on the feet. Lurching away from this scene of defeat. Swaying slightly but otherwise upright and with eyes gradually focusing. On the lights blinking yonder at the dark end of the street. Feeling nausea in the stomach. The throat dry and retching. With a touch of lunacy present. Arising out of incomprehension. The wind's moaning in the ears lacerating the nerves. While a voice in the head wails please God get stuffed. To prove that we are fearless. As we appraise all the faces floating eerily in the ether. Those who once existed but now are stone-cold dead. But have clearly returned to invite me to join them. Which I do not care to do. And so cast them from my mind. And then lean against this wall. To wipe blood from the lips and inspect one's natural molars. Which thank Christ are undamaged. After the recent unnecessary contretemps.

Black night neon-brightened and the growl of passing cars. Lamp-lit pavements showing webs of cracked concrete. Cracked, also, this head of mine. Causing weakness and trembling. And the intimidating threat of an imminent collapse. So now sideways into this jolly packed pub. Where the air is too smoky and the noise almost deafening. But where mercifully the cold beer is quick to stem the sickness. And steady the jangling nerves. Thus defeating the inner demons for another blessed moment. Though no sausage with sauce tonight. Lest we throw it all back up. But compensation in the tits bouncing lightly nearby. Nipples peeking through stretched wool exciting the loins. As we note with the rise. Of manhood's wondrous member. Which alas makes us think. About sexual maniacs. Who cannot do without it and frequently get it. To calm the fears of September years. Now uncomfortably familiar which is why we down this drink. Quickly cooling the palate before back to the street. Agog with suspicion. And the conviction that passers-by are staring strangely at me. So eyes down and guard up. Being fearful acting fearsome. By snarling like a beast causing gasps of female terror. And belligerent male responses. Which are wisely ignored as the streets become familiar. Eventually leading to the house where the postman resides. Stepping lively through the door. Assailed by bright light. And where the eyes of the family turn in his direction. From battle stations.

-Well?

-My dear wife.

-So you're home again.

-Indeed.

-About time.

-Indeed.

-Drunk again.

-Indeed.

-Don't come that one-word superiority with *me*. As if I didn't know you. Drunk as a monkey and trying to act as if you're above the lot of us. Well, you're not. Swillin' our money down your greedy throat and playin' the gent with your flea-bitten friends. What a sight for sore eyes you are.

-I am ill.

-And every week gettin' worse. You hear me? I said *worse*!

-You needlessly repeat yourself.

-Don't you give *me* that kind of talk!

-Aw, lay off him, Mum. He only went for a few pints. Nothing wrong in that, is there?

-You keep out of this, Ross. You're only eighteen and don't know what goes on, so keep your trap shut.

Offensive bitch. Picking on the lad for no good reason. Was always the same and unlikely to change. Insensitive to adolescent sensibilities. Which personally I am not. Being fond of the lad. Who always sides with his dad in moments of strife. And is finally beginning to earn a helpful bit of money. Through his genius at electronics. So perhaps should think of leaving this menagerie altogether. Bravely journey forth to a nice bachelor pad. Taking the lad with me. For the support he can provide. With his generous nature. Which would not mind the expense of this smiling old dad. This being more than one can say for the daughter in such matters. Who being far too sexy and matured beyond her years. Sides with her mother and calls me a swine. Thus giving rise to the anger that I cannot contain. In the knowledge that treachery lurks within. Most women. Something proven this very instant. By two sets of female eyes. Which stare steadily in this direction. Afire with rage and resentment. Compelling me to offer a false smile and defiant repartee.

-Leave the lad alone. He means no harm.

-Don't tell me about my own children. I've spent a lot more time with them than you have.

-It's the quality, not the quantity, that counts. And a meal, preferably hot, right this minute, would not go amiss.

-You'll get no meal tonight. There *was* one, but I threw it in the bin. You have only yourself to blame.

-A meal. Immediately. I am hungry.

-Look at you! All covered in filth! Blood on your nose and cheeks. Like you've been in a brawl and then crawled through a gutter or two. My God! Thank God it's dark! If the neighbours found out!

-Shut your stupid mouth! You hear me? Keep that silly trap closed! I don't return home after a hard day's work to be abused by your foul tongue. So shut your mouth. *Shut it*!

-Christ! Why don't you go straight to bed, Dad? You're just making a bloody fool of yourself. So go get some sleep.

The final insult. From the full and phosphorescent lips of the daughter. Who sits on the sofa in loose-limbed superiority. Smouldering with contempt for this broken old fool. Who nonetheless supports her. Yet cannot properly see her. Because of the blinding rage that suddenly swamps his whole being. And makes him rush forward. With one upraised hand chopping down as he moves. Slapping her face slipping sideways from the chair. With a scream and a thud striking the floor where she now falls. While the wife shrieks you bastard and then leaps toward him. One fist clenched in the air but luckily stopped in mid-flight. By the hand of young Ross who wide-eyed hisses Jesus. And opens his eyes wider as his dad's hand clears the table. Of cups and saucers smashed to pieces and flying apart. This shocking sound blending with the shouting and screaming. Of the Postie and his wife and son and daughter. Spouse shrieking get out while trying to break free from her son. Who is blessed by this fool turning wildly left and right. As he looks for the front door shouting incomprehensibly. And finally finds it and stumbles into the street. To lunge at the silence and sheltering darkness. Where oblique lines of lamp-light paint pale stripes on the pavement. As his echoing footsteps fade away. Into other all too familiar streets.

Passing time leading into this street of dreams. After having been dazzled by the tear-blurred night lights. And stopping off for another drink in a delinquent's dive-bar. Two arguments. One fight. A suspicious policeman's gaze. Then more pavements and brick walls and a crooning cool breeze. As we were carried along like an ant in a flood. Before being cast up on the dry bank of this road. Its silence singing. Its lamps shedding yellow light. Which drips over young lovers and a few fellow drunkards. Who are clearly representative. Of the past and the future. Through which we have ventured in fine thought and foul deed. To arrive at the abode of the widow Peggy Hartnett. Far from the maddening crowd. Knocking gently. Knock, knock. On chipped wood with grazed knuckles. To be answered by a light. Flashing out into the night. From the hallway which is suddenly revealed when her front door is opened.

-Yes?

-'Tis I, the Bogey Man!

-Postie!

-My dear Peggy Hartnett. The moonlit night is filled with surprises. Which is why I am here.

149

-You're drunk.

-How perceptive.

-Christ! Come in before the neighbours see you.

-Damn the neighbours? Who *cares* about the neighbours?

-God Almighty, come in!

Quickly indoors. As the lady demands. Standing briefly in the hallway to aid orientation. Having noted that the walls appear to move in and out. Like a carnival trick. Jigsaws of shadow and light with the patterned carpet sinking. Beneath my booted feet. While a voice in the distance insists that I look a sight. Looking sick, I am told, with my cheeks white as chalk. To which I do not reply, but simply wave a hand. In dismissal. Hoping to show that all is well. Beyond the need for anxiety. Before sinking into this comfy chair. Having removed the coat and tie. Thus proving that the hand is much quicker than the eye. To impress this fine woman who tends to my every need. If not usually with the concern that I now see in her face. This being enough to encourage me to air the closed subject.

-Tell me, dear-heart, is something wrong?

-Wrong, Postie? What do you mean?

-Wrong. Amiss. Your gaze, to say the least, is rather odd.

-I'm just looking at you. At the general mess you're in. Have you been in a brawl? Rolling about the streets? Or was it just another double-decker bus?

-This time a motor-bike. Ridden by an adolescent thug in black leather gear. The streets, my dear, are no longer safe to walk in. But I doubt that the dirt on my clothing is the cause of the expression on your face.

-It's just that I wasn't expecting you. You don't normally come here this night.

And turns away from me. That pale-skinned dark form. Lightly scoring the carpet as she stands on tiptoe. To hang up the one and only coat of the postman. That iron hook on the wall being a better place for it. Than the chair over which it is usually slung. Even knowing, as I do, that I should treat the uniform with more respect. But tending, alas, to great carelessness in such matters. Even if only lately and not without shame. Having once been a gent of fastidious nature. With regard to the appearance. If not too much else. So would certainly appreciate an analysis of this sad fall from grace.

No analysis forthcoming. Since I am otherwise engrossed. In studying the expression on the face of my lady. A touch of anxiety there. With shadows beneath the eyes. Gaze shifting left and right. Uneasily. Over me. As if afraid to acknowledge what it is that she has sensed. My own awareness of this annoying me. And making the teeth grind. Aggravation held in check by the stomach's heaving nausea. While being convinced that a nice drop of whiskey. For the medicinal purposes. Would also help to ward off the multiplying demons. Presently leering at me from the room's four shadowed corners. While sad. And lost. And frightened am I. And suddenly filled with cruel rage.

-A whiskey. Please. I am desperate.
-What happened?
-Nothing.
-You don't usually come on a Monday. Why tonight?
-A few minor aggravations. I can't explain.
-Try.
-Must you?
-Yes.
-Why?
-Because.

Grind, grind. Go the teeth. Rage simmering on the burner. Since we can no longer tolerate the possessiveness of women. An incredibly greedy lot. Wanting to grab hold of their men. Heart and soul, balls and cock. Like cannibals. With voracious appetites. Or like black-widow spiders. First taking pleasure from sex, then making a meal of the donor. It being a chilling truth that man is marked from his birth. As a sacrificial lamb for the so-called gentler sex. Which burdens him with problems. And drains him of ambition. And thus steals his stamina and drives him into an early grave. It being a bitter truth. That most women outlive their men. By behaving like vampires. Extending their own lives by drinking the blood of their victims. These heady contemplations, though fascinating, being out of synch. With the more vital issues at hand.

-Well?

-Alright, I'll tell you. I am starting to suffer from delusions in the night. And from ghostly voices in the full light of day. I drink too much, cough too much, throw up too much, and feel that I'm sliding rapidly into madness. All of this has come upon me during the course of the past few days. It rushes furiously over me. I cannot seem to stop it. And at times I find myself loathing everyone, including my family and you. Now a whiskey. If you will. This very minute. It is desperately needed.

-No. No more drink.

-Pardon?

-Because you're sick enough as it is.

-My privilege.

-And you need help.

-*No*!

The word is out before I can stop it. Like a bullet from a gun. Making her start and turn pale as I blindly lash out. With my booted right foot. Kicking the pedestal lamp. Over onto the floor. The bulb exploding noisily as the paper shade is torn. Spraying the ceiling with light before plunging us into darkness. Out of which her brief scream daggers. As silvery stars stream in circles. Sparkling light on rippling water. This cascade taking place behind closed eyes as I hear myself bawling.

-Bitch! Bitch!

An insult being spat through a curtain of lunacy. Before the raging postman jumps to his feet. To lunge wildly at his lady. Hands outstretched fingers spreading reaching for her. Trying to grab her but missing and staggering on buckling legs. To fall to the floor and scramble about on hands and knees. Coughing. Choking. Finally vomiting most awfully. On the carpet at her feet as she switches on another light. A tall woman. Imposing. Shaking visibly as she stands there. Staring down at the creature staring up from his lowered position.

-Oh, Jesus. *You pig*!

Disbelief and disgust. Her love turning to revulsion. As she cries out the words that she cannot really mean. At this picture of defeat with his nose in his own mess. Thinking Christ oh dear God what have we undone this night? Out of despair and terror. Tormented by the faces of those we once knew. Mocking from the weeds in the green dark tides of time that is gone and forever lost. Haunting. Accusing. A ghostly jury of the mind. Preparing to pass judgement on this prisoner in the dock. Who suffers in the infirmity of age and shattered faith. Which has driven him to violence and unnatural thoughts. Thus turning him into an old, embittered fool. Now succumbing to the delirium of madness and rage beyond reasoning.

-Bitch! Bitch! *You whore*!

And recoil from the words. Which, meaning nothing, destroy all. Whipping and cutting. Scourging that tender heart. Causing her dark eyes to shed gleaming tears. With soft moans of grief parting those moist lips. Which had often whispered words of good humour and affection. Though even now she sank down. To rest beside him on bended knees. And enfold him with her arms. Which she does as he relents. Her tears dripping onto his head. As he buries his face in the bosom that could shield him from sorrow.

-Why? Oh, God, *why*?

And even as his hand is reaching out to grasp a breast, he groans and abruptly turns away. Terror and shame and love and contempt. Sweeping him to the hallway. To the polished brass handle. Which lets the door open to the cold, silent night. Casting him out. Into the darkness. Weeping the tears of a child.

Chapter Thirteen

He slept.

And went down spinning, spiralling, screaming, and emerged to a vastness filled with stars. Here the huge brooding moons still and silent in space, latitudinal lines leading to the infinite. Here the dead and the damned and the anthem of the wind beneath boiling clouds and archways of light. Lines of silver and blue in a streaming rainbow mist over featureless black night and eternity. Falling down turning around and crying out forlornly for help.

Glass rocks, peaks of steel and ridges like molten wax over a great lake of hot ice. Crimson columns of flame divided darkly by more clouds and the ones dying choking within them. With the blood of the lamb dripping into the mouths of the lost ones looking up in despair. His brothers and sisters long departed and now waiting for the blades of the giant skis to behead them. And he pirouetting with elephantine grace while the band struck up playing a gay tune. Much cheering and clapping as the limbs spouting blood were swept up soaking the sawdust beneath. And the ones dying choking in the night in the smoke being whipped weeping help us. To the postman ringmaster in the jockstrap and Wellington boots.

Seeing dinosaurs and serpents and other strange beasts roaming in snow-covered fields. The sun in the sky shining hazed through the gloom on the grey-white of valley and hills. While somewhere the dragon, the spouting, scalding fire, the black-armoured knight on the white horse with wide steaming nostrils.

And the loose-limbed silhouettes running back to the river where the monks fished for human bones and skulls.

Here the flowing was piss and putrescence. Here the sky was a cauldron.

A Dante's inferno where the souls of the departed writhed in a ballet of dread. And under the monks' hoods the skeleton sockets of eyes that had once fed the worms. Ebony smiles from the corpses now dancing on the tombstones in the light of a full moon. With three men lying naked in coffins of wood beneath the father and mother of the middle gent. Hands folded on his chest frozen grin on his face toenails curled up and clean for the last time. Somewhere the mirror reflecting the dead glance in stony-faced wondrous surprise. Six-foot down looking up at the pitiful leftovers, thinking, Well, dear boy, who gives a shit?

Someone, a baby, a boy, an adolescent, in the entry where the cats howled in heat. The cock in the hand of a teenage girl now faceless in the dark flowing out in all directions. Groaning God, God during the hot jolting spasms dramatised in the prism of the mind. Sitting there forlornly staring at himself reflected with his good teeth displaying false charm. Then abruptly the fist rushing forward to the nose which then falls to the pavement badly bruised. And the blood at the fingers poking in gripped by thighs now familiar and slippery in lust. Face to face is the oldest and best way, my dear, though we'll certainly never know until we try.

The burning globe, the teeming darkness exploding.

Bright light and shadow, the whispering trees, the growling of beasts chewing entrails. Here the brute's jaws agape, dripping blood and saliva, looming larger, bending down to further feed. On the tripe of Yours Truly being trailed along the ground to the lair hidden deep in the jungle. Blind panic and rage, razor-teeth at his flesh, scraping sharply on bone pulsing with pain. And then into this quiet place stinking of death and the stench of the limbs not yet eaten. Stretched out on the grass with the stomach torn open being chewed with omnivorous relish. Screaming mercy and then surrendering to oblivion because it's more helpful.

In a glass of amber fluid, tits trembling invitingly, smoke swirling before the eyes and up the nostrils. One hand on the pump squirting semen to the glass by the pint to be swallowed for its goodness. Licking the lips pissing blood and then shitting spermy turds before dropping down dying to the polished floor. Two friends in monks' hoods, both kneeling, kneading fingers, whispering as they slyly steal his wallet. Crawling hoping to escape but the shadows descending as the knife flashes silvery in his eyes. And pierces the windpipe which in letting out air hisses angrily and jettisons life. Gargling throat rattling pumping blood to the sky livid low overhead for eternity. And dying with dignity, friends cackling with mockery, ripping clothes from the barmaid and jumping in. Drunkards drinking pipes piping lewd Bacchanal orgies as the postman is buried alive. In the wine-cellar ruled by giant spiders and fat slick-furred rats.

Here in the vacuum black painted on black devoid of dimension surrounding him. An immense shivering web stretching out to the infinite in oblique lines of shimmering motion. Pinioned encircled by this gossamer web in the heavens with God at the centre. Head bowed in fearful worship and panic supreme as Omnipotence starts scrabbling toward him. From the total dark lair in the middle of the universe where the past meets the present, the finite the infinite, the mortals being mangled in between. And from there at this moment Omnipotence advancing, bloated and hairy growing larger to fill the void, legs multiplying bent multijointed outstretched around eyes popping sideways as expressionless as egg-shells, silence like a storm rapidly building, the belly and arse dropping foul waste over him, writhing in revulsion as the great claws come down, pick him up, crush his bones, stifle screams, and raise him to the wide-open drool-dripping mouth, which then blood-slicked and vile sucks him in, chews him up, and then swallows him without the slightest qualm.

157

He awakened.
Coughing.
Coughing blood.

Chapter Fourteen

Another day. On the beat. Blessed with sanity. We hope. Following a night that was not without its lunacies. Because of the fears which were and are present. With the possibility that the beast which has always lurked within. Has broken loose to drive us to blind rage. And much pointless violence.

Trying to analyse it. Turning it over repeatedly. This way and that. But cannot concentrate. Because of other bleak thoughts. Of other days and far-off years. Which swirl about in the mind to create a storm too dense to see through.

Now walking lethargically toward our street of dreams. Incomprehensibly from the opposite direction. A man needs the change. More so when he feels the ice. In the blood that is pumping this troubled heart more quickly than normal. As I think of Peggy Hartnett. Who might not have gone to work. But instead might still be shedding the tears that she wept last night. Out of love and contempt for the postman on the floor. On his hands and knees most undignified.

Why? Dear Lord, why? What's happening to me? And how will one ever live it down? Particularly at home. To which we humbly returned at the end of the awful evening. With the tail between the legs. Where of course it has always been. But with head bowed in shame. Apologising before spewing into the cracked toilet-bowl. Then back to back in bed with the softly snoring missus. Haunted, as usual, by those spectral beings. Leering mockingly from the far end of the mattress. As I coughed the lonely hours away. And suffered tormenting

159

nightmares. And awakened at dawn feeling peckish.

Alas, now back on the beat. And the weariness has returned. Mind drained and body aching. The trembling even worse. Waves of heat and cold. Vision first clear, then hazy. The street appearing to recede down a long, dark, ominous tunnel. At the end of which mercifully still sits old Pete Whelan. Who is thankfully still alive. And at this moment looks healthier than I feel.

-Morning, Postie.

-Morning, Pete.

-Postie, you look sick.

-Please, Pete, not you as well.

-It's a fact.

-It's a hangover.

-You've got a cough.

-Pete, good day.

And walk on with a blank face. Without showing malice. Although I know that old friend feeling better looks for illness in others. Perhaps in order to make his own forthcoming demise seem more distant. At least until the blood reappears in his white hanky. And the mortal fear returns to be hidden under good humour. Being a gentleman of admirable fortitude. A bona fide True Blue. Which I personally have never been. Nor wanted to be. Having no time for any form of self-delusion. If wanting most desperately to survive. From here to eternity.

Strange thoughts most disturbing. Though no longer unusual. Since, in recent days, such deathly contemplations have gnawed their way into the brain. Causing nightmares and wide-awake fantasies. Plus the vain hope that sex will revive us or offer distraction.

Obviously it's the turning. Of those green dark tides of time without pity. With old age creeping onward like a harbinger of doom. Making one think of coffins or perhaps just closed doors. Which must inevitably open. To let in the darkness we would rather not acknowledge. Though the sun still shines. Over these grey pavements. As I shiver with fear and an odd expectation. Coughing badly but holding down the blood. Scarcely able to force a smile as I greet the athletic twins. Who are cursing in chorus. Under the raised bonnet of their sports car.

-Trouble, gentlemen? A little mystery in the intricacies of modern mechanics? May I, pray, be of assistance?

-Postie, you're being a distraction. And we're both late for work.

-Most humble apologies.

-Jesus, Postie, what happened to you? You look like you've been hit by a bloody bus.

-It was just a bus. There was no blood on it.

-But you *were* hit by a bus, right?

-That's what I told her, but she wouldn't believe me.

-Who?

-The wife. Who else?

-Ah, gee, Postie, you've disappointed us again. The minute you spoke we thought the truth was out at last. With glazed eyes like you have, we could imagine nothing less than a hot bout up the entry with Tina Louise. You in and at her. Wham-bam, thank you, Mam. Come *on*, Postie, give us the truth. Your glazed eyes and stunned expression came out of what caused her departure.

-Her... *departure*?

-Aw, come *on*, Postie!

-I mean it. I haven't heard.

-She left home this morning. In the wee small hours. Carrying a suitcase and flanked by both parents. All deeply grim and hush-hush. Into a taxi and off. We both noticed her red, weeping eyes. And the fact that her parents returned alone shortly after. With mum snarling at dad while shedding her own tears and dad gazing down at his own feet. Very strange, Postie. And now look at *you*. So, you know, it all fits together. And leads us right back to that dark midnight entry, with you, sexy little Tina, and the cats in heat. So, the truth, Postie. How did you manage it where we much younger, super-fit, normally

161

irresistible studs failed?

-Boys, you wrong me. Good day to you.

And off along the street. Deeply troubled once more. Which once would have been unusual but is now commonplace. Finally forced to accept that the poor girl had spoken the truth. Namely, that what they would say would be enough. So deported post haste. Most likely to relatives in some distant safe place. Far from the maddening crowd. With the baby to be born or possibly aborted in secret. Rendered fatherless or murdered. Leaving the young mother with nothing to nurture but her grief. And the silent hell of ostracism.

Because, because. Because of what they would say and did. With help coming from no side. Not even from the kindly Postie. Who in truth was too cowardly to even offer advice. Lest it rebound upon him in the shape of irate parents. Which is why he now feels guilty and mortally ashamed. As he is stopped dead by a foot thrusting up from a low-angled leg.

-So, here we have him! The dissipated postman! One foot in the grave, the other in sexual filth and contempt. And to think that I almost believed in you. What a fool I have been!

Hans Wernher staring up from his seat on the doorstep. Unprecedented malice lending colour to his cheeks. His eyes flashing with rage as he holds up in one hand. A collection of snapshots. Showing ladies with various animals. And the odd bloke thrown in. Direct from the infamous Boogie Street in swinging Singapore. And now being used as evidence against me. Which it is. Irrefutably.

-Mister Wernher. Those photographs. I didn't...

-Too late! Too late! I know where they came from! So tell me, Mister Postman, since I'm dying to know. Did the thought of such filth being opened on my lap really help you to jettison your heavy load? And was it also designed to humiliate this person who was just about to acknowledge your better side? Doubtless it was. And I deserved what I got. For my temporary weakness, if nothing else.

-I can explain, Mister…

-Explanations are not required. My questions were purely rhetorical. In truth, I've always believed that the man who smiles in friendship is merely exposing his teeth to an assailant's knuckles. Well, I smiled and lost my teeth. The lesson has been learnt. Now I know that life's a great swamp stinking too much of human slime.

-*Please*, Mister Wernher…

-Mister Postman, you are mean-spirited and malicious and otherwise insignificant, but you *have* learned how to live in your own jungle, so long may you reign. However, since I believe in giving as good as I get, I'll shortly be sending these photographs to your Senior Postmaster. Given that, I think it's reasonably safe to assume that your expulsion from the service of Queen and Country will be admirably swift. Would you care to join me over a cup of urine?

-Please, Mister Wernher, no more of this.

-Are you whining for sympathy?

-*Shut your damned mouth, damn you, shut it*!

The words are spat out before they can be stopped. A new trait of mine. Decidedly distasteful. Then off along the street with the hasty heart hammering. Shame, rage and bitterness at war with one another. As the breathing comes in spasms and tears spring to the eyes. Humiliating though unavoidable, so what can one do? And to make matters worse. From where she stands across the street. That bitch Missus Whittaker is shouting triumphantly. Mentioning the name of my superior, the miserable Mister Fish. To let me know that she has passed on her catalogue of distorted facts. About perverted postmen and their molestation of innocent children. Not forgetting his being caught peeping through Miss Rigby's mailbox. That unprotected spinster of highly sensitive feelings. All of which, when combined with Wernher's damning evidence, should certainly get me the boot.

And to think that once upon a time I was loved by a needy few. And am presently left to wonder just where I can hide. From the haunting reflection of a face without readable features. Showing nothing but the terror of its own growing madness. So turn sharply left here. Through this open doorway and into stale-air gloom. Mailbag sinking to the floor as we sink into this armchair. Aware of the burning lungs. Wearily raising the weepy eyes. Which eventually manage to focus on good friend Archie Brown. Whose brow is furrowed deeply in consternation at what he is seeing.

-Postie! For Christ's sake! What is it?

-Archie! A beer!

-You're after my breakfast.

-I kid you not, Archie. I'm desperate!

-Something *is* wrong.

-A beer, Archie! For God's sake! *I need it*!

His bewilderment evident in the lines of his sagging face. Before he rushes into the kitchen with commendable speed. To return just as quickly with two cans of lager. Which opened spew foaming froth that drenches his shirt. While I grab a can and greedily start gulping. When not actually spilling it. The hand being unsteady and with no sense of direction. Causing as much of it to splash onto the floor as is poured down my gullet.

Nevertheless, it works. The lager washes down the blood that the coughing is bringing up. And, having done that, illuminates the mind. Casting light on the dark void of the universe within. Which we often explore in sleep but try avoiding when awake. As we are trying to do this second as we stare up at the ceiling. The vision slightly blurred as the pounding heart races. Pumping blood to the brain and down the legs to the tingling feet. Making the toes curl in the boots that now stink with one's sweat.

-Ah, God!

-Postie, listen…

-No.

-You're ill and…

-*No*!

On the feet with the can flying out of the fingers arching gracefully across the room's gloom. At him. Archie Brown. Who though shocked ducks just in time. And straightens up again with his eyes brightly focused. On this fiend of a postman. Who was once a dear friend. And who now in his shame sinks back into the chair. Covering his face. Feeling his warm tears with cold fingers. His head spinning with the madness that cannot be kept at bay. Then in fear drops his hands and opens his eyes and looks up. At the face of the friend whose own eyes are now glazed with shock.

-Jesus, Postie! You threw that can at me!

-I'm sorry.

-You're sick!

-Forget it, Archie. Just tell me about Miss Rigby.

-Miss... *Rigby*?

-Yes.

-What about her?

-Have you seen her?

-Why should I have seen her?

-She's in love with you.

-You've told me that before.

-Don't you care?

-Should I?

-I believe so.

-Why?

-Because life should be offered to the living. And you can help her to live.

Oh, Lord, how pretentious. How ineffably histrionic. The words escaping from the lips in ostentatious humility to fall like lead into the silence. Which resounds with my self-importance and shameless need to impress. Which I find myself doing as a form of self-assertion. Trying to conquer what I sense is the rise of drowning panic. Hoping to stifle my despair at the conviction that all is nothing. A meaningless charade. A spark of inchoate energy in the vast realms of eternity. The present disappearing in the instant of its birth. The future forever just out of reach, though it is always approaching. Every dream and hope rendered superfluous once it is grasped.

All of it meaningless. Or at least so it seems. As I sit here in silence with every nerve shrieking. This undoubtedly brought about by the normal passing of the years. An inevitable occurrence which unfortunately leaves us prostrate. Before our own crippling terror.

-Yes, damn it. Terror.

-*What* was that, Postie?

-Sorry, Archie, it was nothing. I'm just tired. And probably still drunk from my debauch of yesterday. Which has caused considerable damage, don't you know.

-You knocked it back, Postie. You certainly did that. And seem to have been doing it all week.

-How can I deny it? The compulsion has only recently come upon me, but I just can't control it.

-I've noticed.

-Alas, you're not alone.

-I think -

-Speak, physician.

– that you should go and see a doctor.

-Sorry, but no. I simply don't believe in them. And it's just a passing phase. It will pass. You hear? *It will pass*!

-There you go again, Postie. All excited again. You really *can't* keep control of yourself. And it's beginning to show.

-This fucking mailbag. These fucking streets. All the fucking people. This fucking life.

-That isn't the fucking postman talking.

-It is. For the first time.

Silence now. Reverberating. Lingering too long in this small untidy room. Heavy breathing uniting the two fools who face one another. Each avoiding the other's gaze. The one facing the window seeing dusty curtains flutter. To admit oblique lines of shivering light. Which illuminate the motes of dust at play in the air. And make him dwell wonderingly on how small we are. How terribly frail. Too easily broken and difficult to mend, even if clinging desperately to life. By hiding in the shadows of summers lived and gone. Vainly hoping to regain the hope of those distant days. Which being in the past might be no more than dreams. Which repeat themselves endlessly in time and make us believe we're alive.

-Tell me, Archie. Am I mad?

-That's bloody ridiculous.

-I'm not so sure.

-You're sick and depressed. No more than that.

-I need another drink.

-At least wait until lunchtime. If you do, I might even buy you one.

-Can you afford it?

-I'll raid the gas-meter.

-God bless you, Archie.

But cannot move yet. Unwilling to face the streets outside. Reluctant to gaze upon the thespians in this singular drama. The vengeful Hans Wernher. The triumphant Missus Whittaker. The recollection of Tina Louise making me face my own cowardice. Not forgetting Peggy Hartnett, first weeping, then whipped. All of whom, without meaning to do so, flayed the skin from my bones.

So cannot brave their presence. Nor deal with my own emotions. Which, still being flayed right now, make me want to retreat. Both physically and mentally. Searching desperately for a womb. Into which I can crawl. To be couched in the darkness, protected from life's dangers. Thus avoiding the suffering that Miss Rigby knows so well. Torn. By the lack of love. As others are torn by love. Which makes love the greatest destroyer of all.

-I feel murderous, Archie.

-Why is that, Postie?

-I'm not sure.

-Take your bag and finish your beat, Postie. A lunchtime

167

drink should help calm you down.

-Damn the bag. I'll shoulder it no more.

-Come on.

-No. Never again.

-You can't just *leave* it here, Postie.

-I can.

-What about the mail?

-The Post Office will collect it.

-They'll bounce you.

-Let them. There are only two items that I want to deliver now. After that, it's all finished.

-You're raving!

-Perhaps.

Dig down through this bag packed with hopes and heartbreak. Grope around in the wealth of handwritten words to come up with what we need in the hand. One letter. One package. For the young and the old. Retaining enough discipline to avoid ascertaining. The name of the sender on the back of the small, gift-wrapped package.

Instead climb to the feet. Move laboriously to the front door. Where we stick our head out to glance left and right. Along the street. Which is empty. And therefore less threatening. Enabling us to glance back at the old friend and remind him of promises.

-Lunchtime, Archie. In ten minutes. Then the drinks are on you.

-I'm leaving right now. I think I need it. My old postman-buddy isn't himself today.

-Oh, aye. Adios.

Move out with a smile. To be blasted by heat. Of an unexpected ferocity. The sky a white haze. At least this drunkard's eyes. Which do not see very far. If far enough for the moment. Alighting on the house of Miss Eleanor Rigby. Where the curtains are drawn and the silence clings as usual. As we tentatively advance. Treading lightly, with care. Filled with madness and an odd jubilation. And excited by terror.

-Postman, Postman, bring me an aerogramme.

Dear God Almighty! Every nerve-end shrieking. Before realising that this is the voice of a friend. As we do. Eventually. Turning the head to smile at her. With the warmth that we had thought had departed forever. And in seeing her have the feeling that the molecules are dancing. Being gay perhaps joyous in the radiance of her presence. Missus Mary McKay. Aka Miss Lovelorn. Who is one of the last of our links to reality. And deserves the reward that is coming in the shape of this envelope.

-A delightful surprise, Miss Lovelorn. But wasn't quite prepared for your sudden appearance. And why aerogrammes, indeed? The letters are only from Belfast, after all. And in plain white envelopes.

-I like to pretend he's in Singapore or Hong Kong. Or somewhere else nice and safe. It's a self-serving game.

-Sounds like a wise game, my dear. And shows a healthy self-awareness.

-It's a way of keeping sane, Postie. But what's happening? I don't see your mailbag.

-Left it in the abode of the understanding Archie Brown. To come here and join Miss Rigby in a cup of morning tea. Thus relaxing the weary old muscles and enjoying some small talk.

-Oh, please, Postie! *Please* go back and dig out my precious letter. It might be special today.

-Look! I have it here! In my hot little hand. Brought especially for you.

And produce the letter with a flourish. Thus instantly blinding her. To everything but pure emotion. Of the most moving kind. Her face instantly aglow. Eyes wide and bright. Hair tumbling across them in dark, abundant locks. As she snatches the letter. Almost rudely, but laughing. With a touch of trepidation slightly shadowing the radiance of her excitement.

-Oh, God, you're so… No! Wait! If this letter is what I'm hoping for, I want you to hear the news.

Fingers delicate and agitated. Practically tearing open the envelope. Brow furrowed as the letter is withdrawn and perused. Eyes brightening and widening. Breath coming out in spasms. Lips moving as she silently mouths the words that she is reading. Lovely face alive with hope and a fearful anticipation. Before finally turning up to the light of the sun. Which falling upon her blushing cheeks illuminates joy.

-Oh, God, Postie! He's coming home!

The street's silence singing. In the warmth of the blazing sun. Giving happiness to another, the deserving, in this morning of my boundless despair.

Turn aside. Turn away. For such emotion makes us clumsy. She seems more like my daughter than my own and this renders me mortal. Even as she leans forward. To press soft lips to my cheek. And whisper oh thank you dear man before hurrying off. Back to her house to shed tears upon the letter from Belfast. Leaving me alone. Ecstatic. Forlorn. Surprised that she could move me so deeply with her love for another.

-Mister Postman... Here... Please...

A modestly attractive figure. Her face pale and strained. Eyes shadowed by the longing and torment in their brown depths. This being Miss Rigby. The dreamer of dreams defeated. By time and the machinations of life. Now standing in her doorway. A slight, trembling figure. One hand raised in beckoning. Delicate fingers shaking slightly. While the large, liquid eyes shift timidly left and right. Obviously worried about scandal. About those tongues that wag too much. Condemning simple mistakes and making the innocent suffer. And so she now waves her hand. Urgently calling to me. Making me step forward and then stop in front of her. Holding behind my back the package she so desperately wants.

-Yes, Miss Rigby?

-I thought... A cup of... tea, perhaps. I must... Oh, *please*, come inside...

Dimly lit this small jail. With its old, familiar furniture. And a great deal of bricabrac. Polished-glass figurines. Vases filled with withered flowers. One antique radio that is seldom turned on. One leather-bound bible that looks to be well-thumbed. No photographs. No mirrors. Neither memory nor reflection. Having shut out the past and made the future unthinkable. Now spending every day in the silence of isolation. A bleak existence which she hopes to enhance with dreams already defeated.

-Please be... seated.

-Thank you.

-You have... something... for me?

-Yes.

-Oh, dear.

Accepting the package with visibly shaking hands. Turning it over to check the sender's details. Staring intently at it. With a flickering smile. At sight of the name there revealed in blue ink. Then moving back into shadow. Glancing up with eyes glistening. Lips opening and shutting, trying to speak, as a blush reddens her pale cheeks. Then puts the package down. On the table with great reluctance. And clasps her hands in a well-tailored lap where she sits in a wooden chair. Her gaze again lowered. Embarrassed.

-I'll... open it... later.

-Yes.

-It's so... *nice* of him... the gifts.

-Yes.

-It must be so... *gratifying*... to be a... postman.

-Yes.

Shadows shifting around her as her eyes are slowly raised. The silence vibrating from the plucked strings of her anguish. Then a sudden flurry of movement. As she hurries into the kitchen. The clattering of crockery as her nervousness gets things wrong. Before she manages to get things right. And returns with a full tray. While I sit here. Observing. Not attempting to help. As the teapot-spout trembles. Spilling more tea than it pours. On the trousers of my uniform which should be intolerable. Though in this case I bear it. And suppress my senseless rage. Instead trying to concentrate on the rites of civilisation. Sipping tea. Nibbling biscuits. Taking in this odd fantasy. Of life in the pale in a normal living-room. Miss Rigby staring at the package. Resisting the urge to grab it. While I want what she wants. To satisfy my curiosity. By finding out who it is. Who brings her such joy from afar. Being a man. Almost certainly. Probably timid like she is. With perhaps a similar jail in which to hide himself away. While sharing his dreams with her through the post. Where flesh cannot reach.

-Your tea.

-Thank you.

-Sugar?

-No, thanks.

-Well now...

And sighs. In a desperately casual manner. Brushing the auburn hair from her brown eyes. Leaning back in her chair. Glancing at me and then staring at the floor. At her own nervously tapping right foot.

-Miss Rigby, if I may be so bold. Who's your friend?

-My... *friend*? I don't... I mean...

-Yesterday, you were drunk. And clearly crying.

Eyes flicking left and right. Fingers brushing the package. Lips shivering as her cheeks burn again and her head drops in shame. Silence. A deep intake of breath. Followed by a drawn-out, painful sigh.

-Oh, dear... Oh, how awful. How hideous it all is. But I've... *loved* him for so... *long*. And he... I... He keeps *sending* me little things... *nice* things... too shy to give them himself... I don't know... it was just... too *much* all of a sudden. I began to cry at the thought of it. Then... a drink... Something I rarely have... But the pain of... never really seeing him... It was too... too much. And then another drink... And another. Well into the night. And all the time crying... crying like a child... Oh, dear, how can one... *explain*? It just... *happened*. And now I'm so...

so *ashamed*. Yes, ashamed! So, please, I beg of you, tell... no one... Please tell no one. *Please*!

Tears. Rich and glistening. Like green grapes on a white cloth. Her face buried in transparent hands in which webbed veins show. Trembling. Turning aside. Her body convulsing as she weeps. Then sliding her fingers down below her lips to offer a whispered entreaty.

-If you could only... *help* me. *Say* something to him... *You know him so well*!

Sweet suffering Jesus! I don't believe it! Reaching out with a quick hand. To snatch the package up from the table and examine the writing. Familiar. Oh, yes! And then look at the sender's name. Heart racing as we plunge abruptly into a vat of boiling rage. As we see the name written in blue ink on brown paper. Surprisingly neat. Too clear to be ignored. The name of my oldest and best friend.

Archie Brown.

Damn him! No!

And with that I'm up and out of here.

Chapter Fifteen

Damn them to hell. They won't get away with this. Thinking so as he hurries along the sun-dappled grey street. In confusion and fear and a great deal of outrage. For now I can feel it. And all too clearly see. That it was all a huge hoax. Calculated and malicious. Planned by them to derange me and abuse my kind heart. Though will not let it pass. Refuse to give them the satisfaction. The grins to be wiped from their sly, scheming faces. Though here in the sunlight it seems like black night. With shadowy creatures lurking disguised as human beings. Staring at me with spiteful eyes. While choking back laughter. Assuming their victory, but possibly mistaken. Thinking of me as an innocent when in truth I've always known. That they resented my defiance and amiable contempt. As I traversed these streets shaped from concrete, brick and stone. Despising the whole fucking lot of them.

And am not finished yet. No, not by a long shot. Still thinking straight and clear. Very much to the point. And this slick tongue still good for the relevant words. Which they are all going to learn soon enough.

-Oh, Mister Postman!

-Madam?

-I just wanted to ask…

-Please go and fuck yourself. If you know how. Now good-day to you, Madam.

And continue along the street. The pounding heart encouraging speed. Thinking let her put *that* in her report if she knows how to spell the words. Which would make excellent reading for that miserable bastard, Fish. My Senior Postmaster and a son of a bitch. Who just might, after reading it, have an epileptic fit. Thus pleasing the other workers. If not intentionally, decidedly. Though sad to record that I would not be there to see it. The personal resignation about to be tendered. Before we are given the word. Your services, Mister Postman, no longer required. The shame of which we would never live down. If indeed we manage to live at all.

This issue being in grave doubt since awakening last night. Coughing blood and groaning. And sweating like a pig. Recalling the nightmares of death and destruction. Life's underbelly exposed. Mortality raising its ugly head to let us know where we stand. Teetering on the edge of the abyss.

-Hey, Postie!

-Deaf, dumb and blind. Truly sorry. Now please step aside.

Never realised before that the streets are so long. Leading on through exhaustion to some distant shore. Testing limits of endurance. Alas, too soon reached. As they have been with me. Hurt, lost and furious and turning to violence. All dignity forsaken. Realising the folly of trusting the world. Only to be betrayed by mockery, deceit and vile treachery.

Exemplified most vividly by former friend Archie Brown. Who was slapping my shoulder-blades while laughing up his sleeve. At my foolish concern for the tormented Miss Rigby. Whom doubtless he was fucking. Every night like a mountain-goat. In Philistine disregard for more sensitive souls. Such as the postman. Who this second curses him along with some others. Being stung by the knowledge of their secret contempt. And, because of that, no longer frightened of dying. Just so long as I do not go unavenged.

-Hey, Postie, where's your mailbag?

-Up my arse where it rightfully belongs. Now kindly remove yourself from my presence.

Through the entrance to the Post Office. Pride in the stride.

Face grim with purpose this busy hour. Customers in lengthy queues. Many muttering discontentedly. Posting letters paying bills receiving pensions and generally having a hard time. While the eyes behind the counters lift up from their desks. To glance at me in surprise. Taking me in. Minus my mailbag at this unusual hour. Causing Harry to whistle expressively. And Miss Forthright's tits to thrust out as she breathes in. Before the face above the tits blushes brightly and is lowered. Concentrating too intently on the dull tasks on her desk. Obviously trying to avoid my gaze. Having sensed my brimming madness. And aware that the truths too long suppressed have at last been released.

The word clearly being out. Which means I must get into Fish. Before that bastard gets into me. And winner take all meaning pride if nothing else. So across the tiled floor. Around the counter and its staff. Then straight into the office of the Senior Postmaster. Without bothering to knock. The knuckles having had enough practice through the long years behind us.

-Mister Fish, good morning.

-I say, I -

-Be quiet.

-resent –

-My rudeness is my own concern and shall remain as such. Kindly shut your mouth and speak only when given permission.

-By God! Of all the bloody impertinence!

-Impertinence alone. There is no blood on it.

-Damned cheek, you have –

-Quite. And more to come. I stand here to inform you that I have dumped your precious mailbag in the house of a drunken ditch-digger from Deal and I do not intend going back there for it. I also stand here to inform you that my resignation is tendered herewith. I have had just about enough of this menagerie and all in it. Most particularly yourself, Mister Fish.

-Don't think for one minute that *you* can come in *here* to -

-I come in here to bring you self-awareness. The truth hammered out on the anvil. You, sir, are a stench in the nostrils

177

of God, a leech in the side of bleeding humanity. A worm, a snail, a snake in the grass. The bile on the boil of a cancerous arse. You are all of that and less. In truth, you are nothing. One of the living-dead. Wrapped up in red tape and buried alive by bureaucracy. Mister Fish, I pity you.

Impeccably worded. Neatly delivered. Has him squirming in his chair like a man nailed through his balls. Making gargled sounds of protest. Lots of crimson in the face. Particularly in the cheeks bulging under glassy eyes. Gobs of spittle emerging from his straining throat. Choking on his own words.

-How dare you! How *dare* you!

-I dare with consummate ease. Because the object of my attentions has been reduced to its proper dimensions. Less than a spark in the spark of existence, less than a grain of sand on a beach. Yes. Out of the arse of God comes shit smelling of fish. Your kind, Mister Fish, can never really die because your kind have never really lived. The walking-dead indeed. And possibly respected by your own kind. What other kind could respect you?

-Damn you, you're sacked! You hear me? You're finished! And this time you won't talk your way out of it. I have the evidence I need. Numerous complaints, signed and filed. Abuse of children and sexual perversions whilst performing your duties. You're finished, you filthy bastard! You hear me? Never again will you serve a government institution of any description.

-Never again would I want to. Goodbye, Mister Fish. I can't stand the stench in this office, so I'm leaving this instant.

-Swinecuntbastard! *Get out*!

But too late with his abuse. For I am out through this door running sharp as a rabbit. Filled with dread and exhilaration. The unique thrill of daring to cast off one's past. And accept what's to come. Rushing past Harry and the lush creature, Forthright. Tits out breathing in. As wide-eyed she witnesses my escape to the street. Where the noon sunlight dazzles and makes the skin glow. Though also causes nausea and lightness of the head. The legs moving more quickly to traverse heaving pavements. Their magical rise and fall leading to stifled hysteria. Noting that the passing walls are leaning in toward me. As if about to fall upon me. And yet the feet continue marching. In defiance of all. The roaring of cars and their hooting horns hurting the head. Passing unheeding human voices raised in wrath. These pedestrians so ghostlike now parting in panic. Before postmen gone mad in the streets that once seemed so safe.

-Hey, Postie!

-Oh, Mister Postman!

-Hey, you!

Obvious cases of mistaken identity. It isn't really me. It's my doppelganger they're seeing. The one who laid himself down on the altar of life. And was gobbled up by pygmies. Though here and now is his spiritual brother. In flight and pursuit while the bright sky turns grey. Filling up with dense clouds. Which are low and ominous. Reflecting the mood of the mind in its disturbance. Held on high by two legs making getaway motions. At a speed that belies the long years placed upon them. The river dark-running with water mud-slimed. The buses on bridges over barges in snot-spray. Time slipping past out of gear into chaos. Before we turned relieved and with hot aching breath. Into this cool pub for some cheap stimulation. Standing calm behind the counter one thin man in shirt and pants. Face lean and pale and unfriendly. Not too much feeling there.

-Sir?

-Pint of bitter.

-Yes, sir.

Distaste on his countenance. Also contempt. Seeing in the eyes of this customer reflections. Of the uncertain future. Which comes to us all. So pulling the pump with rejection in his gaze. Then sets the pint of beer down with obvious reluctance. Opening his mouth to ask for payment. In the most insulting manner. Which I would like to avenge. With four knuckles and one artful punch. To teach him some manners and get simple satisfaction. But instead drink the pint in a couple of thirsty gulps. And thump the jar back on the counter to display disapproval.

-And another pint, thank you.

-Yes, sir.

Foam white and frothing on amber made golden. By sunlight in beer in which odd shadows lurk. The dead faces leering up from the weeds of days long gone. To be swallowed by the lips down the throat to the gullet. To dull the despair of life's betrayals and torments. Which were painfully revealed to us after the destruction. Of the knights in black armour on resplendent white horses. Aspiring to ideals only possible to the young. Before life's vicissitudes grind them to dust. Leaving nothing but the constant aggravation caused by unanswered questions.

-Sir, I would like an answer.

-Pardon?

-Would you like another drink?

-Yes. Absolutely.

Answers are possible. Though we shy from admitting it. And now suffer revulsion when we sum up a life. As lived on this Earth. Only to end up with a charade. A travesty of what might have been. Flesh, blood and bone, certainly. Balls, belly and arse, yes. But no photos. No mirrors. No true past nor future. Always having lived just for the day. The space between dawn and dusk. Between breakfast and supper with little else considered. Nothing tried, so nothing gained. Except defeat and cynicism. And a future dark with dread because devoid of all hope. To a mind without motive wondering where it all went. And failing to find out facing boundless desolation. As we do. Right this minute. Drinking pints of cooling beer too quickly.

-Barman, good day.

-Good day, sir.

-It was a pleasure.

-Right, sir.

Once more these streets of tar and cement. Concrete and

glass instead of green fields. Deadening the spirit of those living here. Walking on. Urgently. Destination unknown. Passing growling traffic with the passers-by passing. Drab clothes and pale faces. Oblivious to their environment. Strolling lethargically in the boredom of lunchtime in this working-class street.

The timid stepping sideways, eyes lowered, ignored by the bold. Who laugh and talk loudly as they pass one ruined postman. He who now knows that these streets lead to hell. Where the cries of the damned reverberate in the night. And where death comes in small doses. If disturbingly regular. Emanating from the pores in the walls that soar high on all sides.

Shocking thoughts to be thinking. This immemorial day. The nerves lacerated by confusion and fear. Beyond the point of restitution. Knowing that *They* are out to get me. With their fast cars and motorbikes. On which they thunder past with goggled eyes and mad grins. Their machines coughing fumes that cause choked lungs and coughing. Which makes me swell up with a great deal of pity. For old postmen who see madness as their only escape-route. Meaning myself, of course. And my yearning for respite. From the bustle and noise of the life that goes on all around me.

Quickly into another pub. This one more familiar. Offering comfort as one hurries to the bar where the tits seem to smile. Invitingly. Taking deep breaths to confirm it. While with one foot on the rail we flash teeth all our own. Most sincere with the charm. Radiating manly innocence. Hiding the base emotions that rise solidly beneath. The long counter. Where, quivering unseen, it stands up in the pants. While she smiles back with lush lips that could drain it dry. Thus proving that life does indeed go on. Irrespective of wounded hearts.

-Marge, good day.

-Wow! If it isn't the gentleman Postie again.

-One gleaming goblet. Filled with the amber fluid. If you will, please.

-You've been drinking too much, Postie. Just lately, I mean.

-Only an excuse, my dear, for seeing you.

-Ach, away with you!

Pours the pint with a smile. And a most attractive blushing. Titillated by the compliments of this charming old rogue. Who offers entertainment through this otherwise lean period. The pub being almost empty. Which strikes me as a good thing. Since today could not tolerate other babbling human beings. Though can tolerate those tits thrusting forward and receding. Trembling to tease me. Being plump twins of love. In which a man might lose himself. Temporarily, at least. From memories of parents dying choking in the night. Of young girls in entries cold and dark in the past. Where the cats in heat howled in the rubbish at our feet. As we groped and groaned shaking pitifully with lust. On the fringe of adolescence. Before the sperm was jettisoned into the melting cunt. And we matured overnight being married before we knew it. Wham-bam-thank-you-mam, then turning the page to middle age. When you glanced back over your shoulder at your lost younger years. With no dreams left to cherish and sustain you in your faith. White horse blown to pieces. Valiant knight on his arse. Trying to hold back the tears that he wishes to shed. Seeing no farther ahead than the next familiar pub. Where the amber fluid glints seductively. As it is doing right now. On the counter in front of the tits below eyes most perceptive.

-Postie, you're not well.

-Please, Marge, I beg of you. Speak of other things. Such as life, liberty and the pursuit of happiness. And other such unreal matters.

-You say funny things.

-Strange.

-That's what I meant.

-I believe I lust for you, Marge.

-Only when drunk.

-Is that not good enough?

-I don't think so.

-You're a hard woman, Marge.

And she returns to her duties. Pumping beer and pouring spirits. Concealing within her the feminine secret. Of how to face the nightmare without cracking up. As I seem to be doing. With no hope of resistance. Elbows on the counter over cock-hardened lust. Watching her wash glasses and pint-jars and plates. Bent over. Legs long. Skirt tight on a fine arse. Her secret centralised in that area most attractive. To mortal, sensual man. Who would get his face slapped if she knew what he was thinking. If she didn't say yes as quick as you could blink. So might actually try it. And to hell with the consequences. Which could be no worse than doing without it.

-Ah, God!

-*What* was that, Postie?

-I said nothing.

-You did.

-I hadn't realised.

-When you talk without knowing it, it's the end of the road.

-Forgive an old man his eccentricities.

-Not so old.

-Not so young.

Familiar echoes here. The same words spoken elsewhere. By another, more romantic young lady, Miss Lovelorn. Words that now shake me to my very core. Being the words that spell out my mortality. Yet peace be upon us. As the night gently falls. A velvet sheet of solace over life's rampant chaos. As the dark waters rise. To touch the descending sky. Leaving the world suspended in a moment of silence. With one clenched fist upraised. Dry lips murmuring a prayer. Before sinking and disappearing as sea and sky become one. In a darkness that covers the universe blinking out in the dying mind.

-Ah, God!

-*What* was that, Postie?

-Nothing.

-Sounded gloomy.

-It was nothing.

183

-Buy me a pint and I'll ask no more questions. And so save you embarrassment.

Lying friend, Archie Brown. Leaning against my left shoulder. A large man preparing to exploit my generosity. Of spirit as well as pocket. This being a vice I once had to accept. But now definitely resent. More so in the knowledge of his cruel deceptions. The thought of which makes me grit my teeth and control my rage. And instead offer words of a deceptively amiable nature. Before plunging in with both feet and the knife. Which is all he deserves for the tormenting of Miss Rigby. And the betrayal of friends tried and true.

-Marge, a pint. For my good friend here. And one more for me. If you will.

-Bless you, Postie. Behind the wicked smile lurks the soul of a saint. Cheers, Postie.

-Cheers.

-That wasn't an epitaph, Postie.

-I hadn't thought so.

-You sounded so.

-Forgive and forget.

Turning the head to stare at this friend become enemy. If he did but know it, this dissipated, familiar man. Yet now slightly different. Most oddly out of focus. Suddenly false to old memories which themselves may be false. No longer trustworthy so almost a stranger. No closer to me than the numerous other individuals who pass me in the streets every day. White bone gleaming in blood. The skeleton forms. No features to separate one from the other and enable us to pick out a true friend. Which is surely not asking too much.

-Tell me, Mister Brown. Where is Mister Murphy this fine day?

-Lost in the wilderness.

-Kindly elucidate.

-What?

-Explain.

-Oh. He's on a train. Bound for Liverpool. A distant relative died and he goes to pay his respects. With an eye to her will. Which might save him from the horrors of regular employment. So he left this morning. No time to say goodbye. Said to tell you he's going to the moon. And possibly farther.

-Here's to Mister Murphy.

-I'll drink to that.

-I'll drink to anything.

He goes to the moon. And possibly farther. But farther than that is a long way. As he once said to me to make my blood run cold. There being no return from the region of the stars. Where we go when we wander. Off this mortal coil. Eternally lost. Seeking God and His mercy. Revelation and peace. A respite from the trials of life's long travail. Which is being endured this very moment. With the coughing and pained heart. And the feeling that I'm incorporeal. And possibly adrift. Dreaming recumbent on those streams of velvet motion. Floating back through the years. Though the green, rain-drenched memories. To the impossibly distant source of my own being. And the start of the end.

-Postie, what the...?

-*Please*, Archie!

-Christ, you're... *crying*!

-Please! I beg you!

-Postie, stop it! You hear me? For God's sake!

-It isn't me! It isn't me! *It's not me*!

-You're not making sense!

-Christ!

-Postie, go home. Get into your bed. Sleep for a week and ease the tensions. It's all piling on top of you. And you look like a ghost. Not to mention that awful fucking cough. You should see a doctor.

-No!

-Alright! Don't bite! Just a friendly suggestion.

-Liar! Cheat! Manipulator!

W.A. Harbinson

-Who? *Me*?

-Yes, you! Who else? You with your denials and cheap remarks. Who treat that poor woman's love as a joke. With small gifts through the mail. Sent only to make her think that you're a distant admirer. When in fact you're just laughing behind her back. Yes, Archie! *You*!

-What the fuck are you talking about, Postie?

-Damn it, you know! She drank herself sick and right now weeps with shame. Wanting nothing but a word. Which she won't get from you. Unfeeling bastard that you are.

-Postie, you're raving! I don't know what the fuck you're talking about. And look at your hand. It's bleeding! You've just broken that glass, banging it on the counter like that. What the hell's the matter with you, Postie? Have you gone stark raving mad?

-Take him home, Archie. For heaven's sake! He's sick and possibly delirious, God help the poor sod.

-Marge, please. I normally like you, but kindly stay out of this matter. It's strictly between Mister Brown and me.

-Postie, listen –

-To what? More lies? More deceptions? Why not speak instead to Miss Rigby. She *wants* to listen!

-For Christ's sake, listen yourself. You lost me right from the start of this. I wish to hell I knew what you're talking about, but I don't, swear to God. I mean, what's all this about Eleanor Rigby? How did *she* get into this conversation? You're not connecting, Postie. You're not making any sense. So you better go home and sleep it off. For both our sakes.

-You deny it?

-*What*?

-Sending the packages.

-What packages? I don't know anything about any packages! You must be getting me mixed up with someone else.

-*Don't lie to me*!

-I'm *not* lying!

186

-You send her packages! Gifts! Teasing her through the post! Encouraging her to think you care for her! *Damn you, don't deny it!*

-What gifts! You're out of your fucking mind! I don't even send gifts to my bloody mother! You must be dreaming, Postie. Or maybe you're deranged. Either you're getting me mixed up with someone else or you're imagining things. Postie, listen. I'm your friend. Take my advice. Go see a doctor.

-Shut up! You're lying to me! She told me about it herself. This morning! Just after I left you! And I saw your name on the back of the latest package. *I didn't imagine it!*

-You're kidding!

-I'm not!

-Fucking preposterous!

-It's true!

-Well, of all the... Postie, listen to me. It must be some kind of trick. I've never sent a gift or letter to that old bag in my life. You understand, Postie? If you're not having me on, then someone else is. Postie, I know *nothing* about those packages!

-Then it's madness. *It doesn't make any sense!*

-Someone's using my name.

-*Damn you, Archie, just shut your liar's mouth!*

Deeply varnished this door swinging out to noon light on grey pavements paraded by pedestrians. Much pushing and jostling in fume-poisoned air with cars honking over threadbare human babble. Fleeing whimpering inane words. Giving voice to disordered thoughts. Bewilderment turning into fear to make the stomach erupt. A handy lamppost to lean against. As we cough and retch violently. Pavements wavering beneath eyes blurred by tears as we move on again. Singing Onward Christian Soldiers, the mission incomplete. Head spinning with the ringing words of Rigby and Brown. It all being a dream or some kind of hallucination. Nothing real. Nor ever was. Nor ever will be. Yet the riddle still teasing like a cat's eye in the night. Insisting that we have this thing out.

We will have it out!
Breathing harshly as we hurry. Into this sheltering pub. Then from counter to floor on hands and knees as we vomit and shake. Apologising profusely. Humbly begging forgiveness. From the barman well-muscled but devoid of all sympathy. Who picks me up like a rag-doll and throws me back out. Into more streets. More warm pubs.

Time racing past in a dream in a void. Until comes the closing time afternoon sun. Cocoons of white cloud turning grey above the rooftops. And somewhere a dog's bark. The laughter of a child. The sound of a train in the not too far distance. While stretching out ahead the webbed patterns of the past. Streets of dreams, street of dreams. Then this house of dreams defeated. Knock, knock on weathered wood. Waiting patiently until the curtains are drawn apart. Her sad eyes peering out. Into lunacy.

Chapter Sixteen

-Miss Rigby. 'Tis I. The postman.

Deeply drawn the breath. With that frail figure trembling. Slight movement backward, then forward and back again. Dressed darkly discreet. Really rather sweet. Twisting nervous hands patting down lustreless hair. Raising the large eyes which in sunlight show dread. Plus the anguish and yearning for a promise that will never be kept.

-Oh... You.

And again the deep breathing. The flutter of restless fingers. While behind us the street starts surrendering to shadow. A vastly different place in the briefest span of time. Pregnant girls departed, widowed women in tears, soldier-boys from the wars soon returning to love. And alas with a couple of enemies who once were good friends.

So silence. Peace, brothers. As tonight the world ends for the gentle, stricken heart. Here before me the victim. Behind her the altar. A life lived in brick walls concealing. All the hopes never realised.

-Miss Rigby, I must have words with you.

-Oh...

-May I?

-Oh... yes... How *rude* of me. *Do* come in.

Tension in the air. Tingling between us. As I brush against her body passing through. To this dimly-lit jail with its fragile bricabrac. Silent radio on the table. The well-thumbed bible closed. No photographs for memories. No mirrors to reflect an

W.A. Harbinson

unwanted reality. Thus a gloomy but necessary retreat. For one frightened of living.

-Please... be... *seated.*

-Thank you.

-I thought a... cup of... tea, perhaps. I must... Oh, dear, I'm so... *nervous.*

-There's no need.

-Indeed, no. Quite. I...

-Miss Rigby.

-A cup of tea? A sandwich?

-No. Thank you.

-Well, I...

-Please, Miss Rigby, sit down.

-Yes. Well. Perhaps...

Sits gently. As is her nature. Knees pressed together, hands twisting a handkerchief in her lap. Face lowered. Prim. Then her eyes lifting back up like saucers. Suppressed pain now visible.

-Mister Postman, you do not look... well.

-It's nothing.

-You have... worries?

-No more.

-Missus Whittaker has been... *talking* about you. I try not to listen. A most... *distasteful* woman.

-Thank you.

-Pardon?

-For trying not to listen.

-Oh... Yes... It's nothing, really.

-Miss Rigby.

-I want to thank you... again... for your kindness and... consideration. When I... *You* know.

-Miss Rigby –

-I shall never behave like that again. Not even over... *him.* Not ever again. So... *foolish* of me. And doesn't... *help.* Not at all. And the shame... So...

-Please listen to me, Miss Rigby.

-Mister Postman, you cough so badly. And you don't appear to be… well. Perhaps you should visit… a doctor.

-Maybe tomorrow.

-Yes, tomorrow. That would –

-Miss Rigby, I –

-You've lost your job. I know about it already. They were all… *talking* about it. And later, when you left here, they came… the post office van… to collect your mailbag from Mister… *Brown's* house. I cried then… thinking about it… your reasons.

-I spoke to him.

-Oh.

Silence pitched to a degree almost palpable. Making the very air vibrate. With tingling currents humming in this small, uneasy gloom. And all around us the fine figurines of smoky glass. Looking at us with unblinking eyes. Her pain a living presence. Tangible. Real. Hurting both of us like salt on an open wound. And so clearly tortured is her wandering gaze. Deeply-shadowed and nervous. Not knowing where to rest. Almost luminous in the wan face above the slim body. Now lost in the tides of time without pity. And suffering even more because she knows it. Physically expressed through her trembling.

-You understand, Miss Rigby?

-Yes.

-I spoke to him.

-Yes.

-We talked about the gifts.

-Oh, dear.

Turning aside to shiver with embarrassment. And raising the handkerchief to cover her face. Eyes glistening above the white cloth stained by wet lips. Staring blankly at the wall. On which hang no paintings, no photographs. Breathing harshly in erratic, strained spasms. Her soul wounded. Torn.

-Miss Rigby.

-Yes.

-Mister Brown claims no knowledge of the packages.

Tears. Clinging glistening to the rims of the wide eyes. Then dribbling down the cheeks. To fall upon the pursed lips. Forlorn. Exposing grief. As she sobs into the handkerchief. Her weeping muffled. Though the shaking reveals what she is suffering. Shame. And despair. Love's anguish and futility. Dreams not only defeated, but lost. Beyond hope of recovery.

-Miss Rigby. The gifts. Who sent them?

Inward drawn the breath. Released again with the confession. Whispering

-I did.

-To yourself?

-Yes. Oh, God, yes!

-Why?

-I don't know. *I don't know*!

Leaning forward face down. On the faded flowery sofa. Lightly beating her clenched fists into the cushions. Body quivering like a reed in the wind. Sobs rending the room's lacerating silence.

-Miss Rigby. Please. Don't.

Then compassion and outrage. Tension and heat. The walls disappearing from a narrowing range of vision. With darkness closing in around a web of striated light. Heart pounding. Throat choked. Moving forward in a trance. Someone. Not me. Not the sickening postman. Someone else. With intent. One hand outstretched and falling. To touch. Her frail shoulder. Then the fingers through her hair. Exploring neck, throat and eyes, that narrow, yielding waist. And taking hold. Tentatively. Carefully turning her to me. To see her look up entreatingly. Lips opening and closing. Before whispering the shocked words:

-You touched me!

-Yes.

-Oh, please, don't!

-Yes.

-Oh, God! God help me! *Please* don't!

Closer. Still closer. Her wan face looming larger. Eyes

alight with dread. And with helpless anticipation. Shadows falling on her cheeks. My shadow. Someone's shadow. Both breathing more harshly. With raw nerves and tension. In the silence of this sadly gloomy room.

Then a sudden, violent, relentless outpouring. Of something much greater, more lasting than themselves. Flowing down and around them as a cloak against the storm. Great pity and love. Desire and the need to share. Self-consciousness dissolving in the heat of the moment. Crying out. Groaning. Lips brushing at lips. Body arching over body on the couch quietly squeaking. Fingers pressing a soft breast. Which trembles like a dove. The blouse falling from her shoulder. Brassiere sliding off the breast being pressed by his rough hand. Wet tongue on a nipple for a scorching, hopeful instant. Before the body on the couch twists below the one on top. And with hands attempting to push him away she cries the single word:

-*No*!

Making him freeze above her. Unable to move. Petrified by shock and frustrated desire. Looking down to see her large eyes bright with panic looking up. While frantically tugging the blouse back up over her breast. Then a trembling passing through her. The rising shame of her own desires. And he filling up with bitterness. With rage and contempt. All stirring in the pot boiling over with pity. For her. And for him. For the world that divided them. Then staring down into her haunted eyes. To ask the question that could never be answered.

-Why? *Damn it, why*?

-Oh, Lord! Oh, the shame!

-*Why*?

-It's too late! Can't you see that? I don't *need* this anymore! Only love. And wanting to be wanted. But this? *It's too late*!

-Bitch.

-No!

-Cock-teaser.

-No!

-Slut.

-*No! No! No*!

Slumping back on the sofa. Hands covering her face. Shadowed and shaking as her weeping rends the silence. Whipped raw by the postman who straightens up and slips away. Feeling triumph and shame simultaneously. Before feeling nothing.

-Miss Rigby.

-Get out! Get out!

-I'm going.

-Oh, no! *Please*!

-Please *what*?

-Stay awhile.

-What for?

-Because… because…

-Stop crying.

-Please stay! Just a little bit longer!

-There's no point, is there?

-There is!

-What?

-I don't know!

-Goodbye, Miss Rigby.

-Please, God… *Help me*!

-I can't help myself.

Slam. Goes the door. Behind him as he leaves. Locking in the damned. And setting himself free. In the afternoon's grey light and lunacy. Stumbling drunkenly on pavements. Tears staining his cheeks. Sensing demons all around him lurking leering in the shadows. As out of his throat comes a cry of defiance. Which instantly breaks down into coughing and a much deeper sickness.

-*I am not insane*!

For this is not me. It was never really me. It was merely a nightmare on the brink of awakening, a drunkard's recurrent tormenting dream.

Listen! I am real. I exist absolutely. I have a past and a future and I *can* perceive the present. Chest aching throat burning to prove that I exist. So listen! I have a family. They are part of me, also. I once penetrated young flesh and out of my seed sprang the stirrings of life other than my own. It was not a dream. And nor am I dreaming now. I saw, I touched, and I knew. As I know at this moment.

Yet where are they now? And, indeed, where am I? For I can neither remember where I am going nor why I am walking.

-Oh, dear God, I *am* mad!

Listen! Hear my words. Read what my mind transcribes. This is my street of dreams in late afternoon. A normal place where life foils the living. I recognise each door and I know every name. Though my memory is tripping unsurely through fog and leaving me lost in confusion.

The coughing. The pain. The taste of blood in the throat at last. Yet I'm certain that I'm not mad. I am *not* mad! *I am not mad*! It is merely the exhaustion of illness and fear. I recognise each door and know who lives behind it. And can certainly recite all their names as proof of my sanity.

To the front is the house of Archie Brown, a friend betrayed by my lack of trust. Farther along is the house of stunted Hans Wernher, an ally betrayed by my malice. Obliquely lies the house of the widowed Peggy Hartnett, a mistress betrayed by my blind rage. When I see them I will know that they are real and shall harbour no doubts.

-You understand? *I am not insane*!

Walk on. Walk on. Let your thoughts find their voice. Let them ring out loud and clear in your mind and vibrate through the cosmos.

Can you hear me? It was all an accident. Of blinding fear and the need for vengeance. Had I understood my own dread I would not have lashed out. At those whom I loved who were nearest at the time. It was the fear I had to kill – not the warmth of the friendships. It was the pain I had to kill – not the kindness that was often showered upon me. And the dread and anguish that were so long suppressed. Haunting me then and still tormenting me now in the gloom of this afternoon street. While I cough and choke and swallow my own blood. Walking on. Walking on. Seeking faces that hide behind curtains and refuse to reveal themselves.

-*Help me*!

No light from this window. No sound from this door. Behind this brick wall is a silence where laughter once reigned.

Peggy Hartnett, where are you? My lady, come to me. Please help me I'm cold in the street at your door with the blood coming up from my lungs. Cough, cough. The blood is warm, wet and bright, and it's draining me, please God, Peggy, where are you?

No answer. No word. No sign of forgiveness. Oh, where are you now that your tears have ceased?

But no light from this window. No sound from this door. As the postman hammers knuckles, knock, knock, on the door. Even as he coughs up more blood and suffers his final guilt.

-Drunkard! Degenerate! Hammerin' on your whore's door! Givin' away what decent folk knew all along! And cryin' like a child! Like a stupid wee girl! Why don't you go home and confess yer sins to yer wife? You might as well, 'cause believe me, you'll molest no more childern in this street. So go on! Be off with ya!

Bitch! Witch! Foul-mouthed fat whore! Triumphant and bloated on the pavement arms crossed Missus Whittaker Pig-Features the First. Oh, Jesus! Oh, God! Turn away from the sight. Of that vulture who pecks greedily at the wounded and defenceless. And continue retching badly en route to more hopeful climes. Along this wall of closed doors. Past curtains fluttering furtively and shedding their dust. Turning in to knock loudly on the door of an old customer. Who should have been a friend. Crying help me please help me and do not accuse with that silence more damning than words.

-Wernher! For the love of God! *Wernher*!

Silence. Resounding. And lingering too long. Then eventually the mice-like scuffling of movement within. Someone quietly retreating to the back of the front room. Refusing to help. *You're only a common postman with delusions of grandeur...* No, I will not accept it! This crude, brutal, ironic form of retribution. So knock, knock. On the door. Hammer, hammer. With the knuckles. *Care to join me over a cup of urine?* No! I won't let myself sink. To the centre of the Earth. *And farther*. Definitely not. Since farther than that is a long way, indeed.

-For the love of God, Wernher, answer the door!

-*Does the wise man quote Socrates to the monkey*?

-Damn you to hell, Wernher! Damn you!

Listen! Please listen! These are first and final words. It wasn't really you that I sought to humiliate, but your superficial, less worthy half. It wasn't really you whom I wished to defeat, but your more inhuman, supercilious twin. Life is the Grim Reaper chopping all down, and you and I are merely his victims. So smile at me speak to me offer forgiveness before the night lowers its heavy curtain. *You have the pavements at your feet, no more*. No more. And the blood that I taste in my throat now soaks my numbed lips.

-*Damn you to hell, Wernher, damn you*!

Shriek now at the afternoon's grey desolation, at the pavements leading only to other closed doors. Shriek your rage and defiance, releasing grief and panic, with a fist clenched and raised to the sky. Salt in the eyes, a burning in the chest, a cold wind whipping your futile words back to their source. But shout and rage. All is not lost. Courage can be drawn from contempt and give strength to the weak.

-You hear me? *I don't give a damn*!

To whom can we turn? Where do we hide? *Down in the pub where the twin tits smile*. The house of Archie Brown. Betrayed by lack of trust. *Buy me a beer. Forgiveness forthcoming*. Lights out and door shut. No sound from within. Knock, knock.

W.A. Harbinson

Hammer, hammer. Dear God, Archie, answer. *Being a postman you'd know. About such things...* World's End. Desolation. Day fading into night. Bringing gloom and a garland of memories to cherish. Regarding the vain hopes. The unrealised dreams. The inanities of life on an Earth that nurtures only the dead. *If clues were shoes I'd be barefoot.* And much better for it. But dear God, please God, send an answer before I start screaming.

-Where are you all?

They hide behind walls, in the streets, in the pubs. They hide behind forlorn dreams, in lost hopes and inchoate yearnings. At least so he now believes, having lost touch with his own history. Aware that a war is raging and a wild beast is at large. Daring onlookers to laugh at this drunken fool dying in the gutter. Minus his mailbag.

So, mercy. Mercy! From a stranger's helping hand. To the gentle heart bleeding. Pierced to the quick. Torn by grief for the past and fear of the future. All else washed away beyond hope of redemption. *Flesh of my flesh. Blood of my blood.* But where are they now? And why did I betray them? They are sitting at home, discussing my insane flight, not aware that I'm stumbling in the night's descending darkness, feet soaked in the water in the gutter that reflects the pulsating stars. And now tripping and falling. Rolling onto my back. Closing my eyes to that sparkling sky. And hearing my own voice from faraway. A murmured plea to the heavens.

-Help me... Someone... Please.

-Postman, Postman, bring me an aerogramme.

Auburn hair over brown eyes. Perfect teeth in a nervous smile. Floating below the sky high above the dark clouds gathering beyond the mist materialising from the ether. Looking down upon me. Miss Lovelorn clearly concerned. Offering quiet words of compassion.

-Mister Postman! What happened to you? I heard you shouting. And saw you fall. Please try to get up again. I can't lift you. You're too heavy. *Please!*

Too late. Alas, my love, too late. The mist deepens into something darker than light and only your anxious face remains.

A lovely face. As is your nature. As some of us are at certain times. Time suddenly passing too quickly and leading to silence. While I drag my feet across the pavement, arm around her willing shoulders, then black out and recover in this small gloom, lying on her settee.

Alas, my love, too late. Since this silence is my sentence. Thus calm and at peace do we finally drift away. From the nightmare. Smiling. The racing heart slowing down. The coughing reduced to faint murmuring in alien regions. *I'm not gentle, I'm tired. I'm not fatherly, I'm old*. And wonderful for it. *Curling the toes*. And happy to do so. In deep, dusty armchairs with exposed, broken springs. No need for fear. Calm acceptance. Simply taking it all as it comes.

-I think it's bronchitis. He should have seen a doctor a week ago. Please, Mister Brown, ring for a doctor. Quickly. Oh, quickly!

Don't cry, Miss Lovelorn. Your tears are not required. There is no pain and little need for grieving. Yet the tears falling glisten. And dazzle me with their radiance. And remind me of the love that links us all at one time or another. *It wasn't that I feared death*. But merely that he loved life. *Which gave me certain inalienable rights*. Admittedly abused. Though rarely with malice. Or the lack of good humour. A million years ago. Long before the mists appeared. And changed into something much darker than light. Strange and enchanting to the unravelling mind. In which the universe is reduced to the pupils in brown eyes. Now anxious and still filled with tears that resemble the stars.

-Mister Postman! Can you talk? Please! It's me! It's Miss Lovelorn!

Rain falls on green fields. Rivers coil toward distant horizons. Black-winged birds glide under webs of striated sunlight. Which touches us. Tenderly. Melting the useless body.

As smiling we look up, our tears dried by this new day. Now knowing that tomorrow always comes and will stay with us always.

-Oh, doctor, thank God you're here. I think he's really bad, really sick. Can you help him? God, help him!

Alas, too late, my love. The time for helping has been and gone. Because help is for the living. And from that I retreated a long short time ago. When you and I were young, Maggie. And daffodils danced freely. As they do again right now. Forming a rolling sea of white and yellow. On green fields now wavering in shimmering heat-waves. Which resemble your warm breath. And remind me of your presence. Under this great sky. A vast sheet of azure blue. With the black-winged birds gliding. And singing on high. As always and ever. On the long road to eternity. In the space that forms a bridge between past and future. And which must be traversed. Pain the premium on peace. Truly a bargain. When all is said and done. And the curtain comes down for the final time.

-Too late, Miss.

-*No*!

Faces spinning above. The ones I never really knew. In the green dark tides of time gone and vanquished. Displaying a little fear. And a certain curiosity. With the weeping of one who might love me. In her fashion. For my gentle smile. And tender, wounded heart. Now cast adrift and maybe lost on the road to twilight. Far from kith and kin. Yet back to back with the wife. *He's my son and that must count for something*. With pink paint to knowing lips. *Yeah-yeah and doodeedah*. Maybe we're strangers. As most of us seem to be. To each other calling hopefully. Across the Great Divide. Filled with hopes and aspirations. And dreams that could come true. When a man eventually comes to the September of his years. And realises that you can't go home again. And wouldn't want to, dear friends.

-Doctor! He's coughing blood! *Doctor*!

Faster now. Faster! Drifting backward on the back along

velvet streams of motion. The memory of female lips blessing the growth. Of the soul in its full flight. Soaring to glory in this great sky that sweeps out to eternity.

-Postman, Postman, bring me an aerogramme.

A fine morning today. Crisp. With the sky a kaleidoscope under a radiant sun. Morning, Madam! And don't forget the smile. Fifteen-carat and then some. Sprightly now! Along these pavements. And into my street of dreams. Defeated, never. Defiant, ever. With springs in the shoes and a song in the heart.

Tralala-doodeedah. Humming sweet melodies with sour breath. So beware, beware. The postman's knock. And no filthy remarks. On the door. Knock, knock. And smile. Again. With the healthy molars glinting. Before you get a mouthful. Of troubles not your own. Then Onward Christian Soldiers, the mission incomplete.

Mister Murphy? Mister Brown? How are you? Okay? And a sausage with sauce. And a pint of the best. For the medicinal purposes. No more, I assure you. And to hell with this mailbag. And everything in it. So cast off this dead weight. And damn the consequences. Out of the street of dreams. Into the misty fields. Now treading lightly, with sublime, balletic grace. Because tits. And grand ones. Are the reasons, my dear. Dearly beloved. All of you...

You and I.

So...

Wow! Yippee! Three cheers for the living. And lewd thoughts this day. Small comforts to a singing man. Walking on. Moving forward. Into the dawn. With perhaps an intrigue to brighten the way. Since a man needs the sustenance. Also must celebrate. End of a weary week, after all.

Oh, you!

Oh, me!

Oh, my!

Knock, knock.

Epilogue

-*He's dead.*
-*No!*
The girl laced her fingers across her face and wept the tears of a child. She had thought about death, often knowing it in her dreams, and at last it had come to her door. This charming old man with the quick-silver tongue, now gone with no family to grieve for him. Only yesterday smiling, now dead, sucked back into eternity. Had he known when he laughed with her? Had she looked close enough to see? He had been dying, dying, all of that last week, and nobody had remotely realised. Oh, Lord, the shame! Oh, God, the horror! How could he have departed before her very eyes with late-evening sunlight on his face? His hair was streaked with grey, his bright eyes were lifeless, and his gentle smile was frozen on his face. What had he thought? What had he felt? How had he actually lived that final week? The girl wept while the armies of pain tramped over her stricken heart.

-*Miss, if you wouldn't mind, please sign these forms. As a witness.*
-*I'm married.*
-*Of course. Now the forms, please.*
The doctor was busy and a bit short on patience. This was a troublesome case and might take some time. No name, no identity. The street simply knew him as Postie. The doctor would have to ring the head office and check on the postman's employment number, and from that they could ascertain his name. Such being modern society. Organised. And the doctor

203

neatly gathered in his papers.

    -Please stay outside.

    -I live here.

    The young man had a lean face with wary hazel eyes and a certain amount of unburdened fear. His soldier's uniform was strangely at odds with the small, neat stillness of the room. He was obviously confused by what he was finding here as his wife looked up, and saw him, and let loose a gasp of disbelief. Then she was sighing and weeping in his arms, holding him, bringing him home, as she had done so many times in her death-haunted dreams.

    -Oh, God, thank you, God!

    -What the ...?

    The curtains shivered and the light expanded, illuminating motes of dust at play. Milling outside, the neighbours were curious; the ones inside were shocked and disbelieving. A bewildered glance from the young man in the soldier's uniform, an anguished wailing from the girl in his arms. Somewhere a sports car roared. And nothing stood still.

Afterword
by
Colin Wilson

I first encountered the work of Allen Harbinson in 1973, when a newspaper sent me a review copy of a novel called *Instruments of Death* (American title: *None But The Damned*). It looked distinctly unpromising – with a lurid cover showing blazing tanks and bursting shells. Most war novels are a form of mild pornography: tales of mass murder and devastation that produce the same ambiguous effect as descriptions of rape. So I began reading in a spirit of clinical detachment – mainly to see whether it would be as bad as I expected. It took me only half a dozen pages to realise that, whatever the author's intention, it was not to shock or titillate. He was frank about the hero's problems – sexual and otherwise – but it was with the painful honesty of someone determined to tell the truth at any cost. And the hero himself represented an interesting new departure.

There have been plenty of novels about sensitive young poets and artists struggling to achieve self expression and plenty of novels about working class lads fighting for a place in the sun. This was the first time I'd read a novel in which the hero was 'artistic' *and* typical working class. Joyce's Stephen Dedalus and D. H. Lawrence's Paul Morel may be working class, but they are not typical; they seem to be disguised aristocrats. Allen Harbinson's Johnny Ramsden believes that he is 'going to be a poet or die', but he has no idea of how to go about it; to escape

205

the drudgery of work in a foundry, he joins the army – and finds himself in another kind of trap. Then the war begins – offering him the most insidious kind of false freedom...

I must admit that the novel aroused unexpected feelings of nostalgia. I was eight years old when the war began, and I was in Leicester, not London. But I can still clearly remember that atmosphere of excitement and patriotism, and the slogans like 'Walls have ears' and the songs like 'We're Gonna Hang Out the Washing on the Siegfried Line', and the films like *We Dive at Dawn* and *The Way to the Stars*, and the marvellous certainty that the Allies were on the side of the angels and the Axis partners were murderous criminals. (The Russians were also murderous criminals at that early stage, but they soon repented and joined the crusade against fascist barbarism.) From a child's point of view, the war years were a good time to grow up in. There was a marvellous glow of optimism, the feeling of shared danger, and a pervading atmosphere of romanticism not unlike that of certain Hollywood pre-war epics (*Robin Hood, The Prisoner of Zenda*). Black was black and white was white, and we were all one happy family. Even for a child, the news was always interesting; it was rather like a world-championship prize fight or a Cup Final soccer match that went on for five years. All of this came back to me in a rush as I read *Instruments of Death*.

I wrote my review, and in due course met the author, who was the Chief Associate Editor of two male-interest mass-circulation magazines (*Men Only* and *Club International*). My first sight of him was a shock. I'd expected to meet a middle-aged Fleet Street professional; in fact, he looked like a teenager who'd run away from school. What was even more astonishing was the fact that he was obviously too young to remember the war. (He was born two years after it began.) He was slightly built, with a friendly but shy manner, and the abstracted look of the born idealist. It seemed incredible to me that this man should have been capable of such a major feat of imaginative reconstruction of wartime England (particularly since he was born in Belfast). What seemed even more astonishing was that he was the thoroughly competent literary editor of two of England's largest-circulation magazines.

During the course of the next eighteen months, I wrote a few articles for the magazines, and spent some hours in Fleet Street pubs drinking and talking with Allen Harbinson. We did at least as much talking as drinking, for he is not the hard-boozing journalist type. And it dawned on me that he may well represent a new species of writer.

We have seen many interesting changes in this century: first, the generation of the great didactics – Shaw, Wells, Chesterton *et al*; then the dedicated Artists – Joyce, Pound, Eliot; then the leftist poets and novelists of the thirties; then the 'Angry Young Men' of the fifties. Each generation seemed related to the age that produced it; Shaw and Wells to post-Victorian optimism, Eliot and Joyce to post-war pessimism, Auden and Isherwood to an age of political ferment, the 'Angries' to an age that saw the disintegration of the British empire. And what happened then? The younger generation took over; protest became fashionable; the economy boomed; computers became almost as common as motor cars and rather more common than bicycles. The technological age predicted by Wells and Jules Verne had definitely arrived. But where were the new writers? There were a few highly talented film-makers – Kubrick, Antonioni, Ken Russell – who reflected the new tempo. But no writers.

Now Allen Harbinson, it seems to me, is a typical writer of the seventies: not so much in the subjects of his books as in his attitude to the craft of writing. To begin with, when I asked him what writers had influenced him, he explained that he had been influenced less by writers than by film-makers – in his early years, the major American directors, more recently Kubrick and Russell. He feels at home with the cults and fashions of the past decade in a way that I never could. (He is the author of books on Elvis Presley and Charles Bronson.) He is a sensitive and intelligent writer, yet he has battled his way into literature as Balzac did – by churning out potboilers. He admits he finds it something of a strain to edit two mass-circulation magazines and write his own books – yet he does it with quiet efficiency. I find the mixture incredible; it is like trying to imagine Stephen Dedalus editing *Playboy*. But then, Balzac and his contemporaries seemed to find it natural enough, and I wouldn't be in the least surprised to encounter a character like Allen Harbinson in *Lost Illusions*.

A biographical sketch may underline the point. Like his own Johnny Ramsden, he left school at the age of fourteen, worked in a textile factory, and studied to be an engineer at night school. Two more years were spent in Birkenhead as an apprentice gas-fitter; then he decided to emigrate to Australia. There, in Sydney, he worked in Woolworth for a while, then joined the Royal Australian Air Force. He saw something of the Far East, was in Malaysia during the Indonesian crisis, and finally returned to Belfast at the age of twenty-five.

By this time, he was already a commercially successful writer. In one hectic weekend in 1966, he produced no less than five short stories, and four of them were sold to an Australian magazine. Convinced now that he could write, he persuaded a paperback publisher to give him a contract, and produced five novels ('mostly comedies'), each about 35,000 words. The first was written in two days, the second in a week, and the third and fourth in the evenings of two weeks.

I do not know whether it is easier for a writer to find publishers in Australia than in England or America; if so, then Allen was lucky, for the greatest problem for all writers is to 'get started' – which is a matter of confidence and hard work rather than literary merit. Shakespeare, Moliére, Ibsen and Brecht all served an apprenticeship during which they 'tinkered' with other people's plays and gained the confidence and technical ability to write their own. Nowadays a writer has to produce a competent novel or play before he can even make a start; the system probably strangles an enormous amount of talent at birth.

Allen's hack-work actually enabled him to produce his first serious novel, *The Running Man*, set in a sleazy rooming house in Sydney. And when I read this – for the first time – recently, I found it fascinating because it is obviously a 'bridge' between his potboilers and his serious work.

The hero – an Australian would-be writer – leaves home and tries to become anonymous in the King's Cross slums of Sydney. He is unsuccessful; the other tenants are friendly and curious, and he is soon introduced to the hero-villain of the novel, Jack Collins, an Aborigine pimp. The writer is fascinated by this dominant, ruthless character who, in spite of his racial disadvantages, is obviously making his way in the world. With a certain cynical amusement, he tells the narrator that he is providing him with materials to write about. (This is after a particularly revolting session with a middle-aged prostitute.) The jibe turns out to be truer than he thinks. Collins kills a man in a brawl, and his own downfall provides the subject of the novel. Collins enjoys playing Svengali to a self-destructive alcoholic (with whose sister the hero is in love). He pushes the alcoholic too far; he eventually hangs himself. And when the police come to investigate, Collins assumes they have found out about the murder, and shoots one of the detectives. He, in his turn, is shot to death. The hero then embarks on a month-long bout of alcoholism, but decides it is time to stop running, and returns to the girl...

The plot is melodramatic and at times incredible, but the novel has real power and conviction. Anyone who bought it off an airport bookstall for the sake of the sex and violence would quickly realise that the author is a genuine writer, not a commercial hack.

The book may have produced the same conviction in Allen Harbinson; at all events, he now returned to a war novel he had started eleven years earlier, at the age of eighteen, and set out to transform it into the story of another 'running man', told against the panoramic background of the Second World War. In a sense, he was following the advice of T. S. Eliot, who once said of Joyce's 'mythical method' in *Ulysses*: 'It is simply a way of controlling, of ordering, of giving a shape and a significance to the immense panorama of futility and anarchy which is contemporary history'. Allen Harbinson chose the myth of the world war – for by now, it *is* a myth – and used its 'futility and anarchy' as a background for his story of a working-class intellectual trapped in a society he loathes. Again, he pivots the novel on the relationship of the introverted hero and a cynical, hard-bitten opportunist, Beatty. 'If the fool would persist in his folly he would become wise,' said William Blake, and in this novel, we watch Beatty persisting in his opportunism until it disintegrates under the impact of reality. With the death of Beatty, Johnny also disintegrates; but the novel ends with a suggestion that this collapse will lead to a new birth: 'Tomorrow – who knew? – he might reach once more for the stars. But today he would sleep away his pain.' What now emerges with unmistakable clarity is that Allen Harbinson is basically a moralist.

It seems a pity that a book as remarkable as *Instruments of Death* had to appear as a 'paperback original'. Yet in another sense, it underlines Allen Harbinson's most interesting quality: the ability to write a serious novel that can also hold the interest of a mass-paperback audience.

In the twentieth century, the serious artist and his audience have been drawing farther apart – and I use the word 'artist' because this includes painters and musicians as well as writers. A century ago, the writer, the painter and the musician could all appeal to 'the man in the street' and still express their deepest intuitions; nowadays, the serious artists are too 'difficult' for the man in the street, and the popular artists are too trivial to be taken seriously. We have two kinds of writer, two kinds of painter, two kinds of composer: 'popular' and 'serious'. And this situation is disastrous. Because the 'serious' artists are difficult

210

for the wrong reason. Not because their ideas are too *complex* for the average reader or listener, but because they themselves are suffering from a fragmented sensibility, an inability to create the kind of integrated structures that came naturally to Balzac and Hugo and Wagner. In short, because they tend to be self-divided and neurotic.

It has always been my conviction that the 'outsider' has to develop the strength to become an 'insider': not by capitulating to a corrupt society, like Balzac's Lucien de Rubempré, but by deliberately using the techniques of the 'insider' to make himself acceptable. As far as I know, Graham Greene was the first serious modern writer to deliberately use the techniques of the thriller to achieve a wider audience for his ideas; few have tried to follow his example. Allen Harbinson has done it instinctively. But, unlike Greene, he is not a pessimist. There is no life-rejection about *The Running Man* or *Instruments of Death*. And for me, the most interesting feature of *Knock* is the development of this underlying optimism.

At first sight, *Knock* seems to be a retrogressive step in the author's development. It is an 'experimental' novel, told entirely in terms of the stream of consciousness of its central character, a London postman. But within a few pages you become aware that, in another sense, the writer has taken another step toward the ordinary reader. If Johnny Ramsden is Allen Harbinson's Stephen Dedalus, then the postman of *Knock* is his Leopold Bloom. He is kindly, easy-going, lecherous and funny. He is also fascinated by the life that goes on around him. The novel describes – or presents – the last few days of his life, and the events are both tragic and funny.

The postman is married to a nagging wife; he is having an affair with a middle-aged widow; and he feels a strong sentimental attraction toward the gentle and sad-eyed Miss Rigby. (It is typical of the author that he should pay this oblique compliment to the Beatles.) He also feels varying degrees of lust toward various young girls encountered on his round. But Miss

211

Rigby means more to him than these other objects of casual desire; she seems to represent something he has missed, something essentially gentle and feminine. At one point, the postman is convinced she is in love with him; only to discover that she is in love with another man, and has been writing herself letters with his signature. The collapse of his daydream is accompanied by a physical collapse – he has been working with bronchitis – and the novel ends with his death.

After the brief introductory section – which takes place after his death – the reader might be forgiven for assuming that he is about to be treated to a Beckett-like sermon on the futility of life. In fact, if there is a flavour of Beckett in this novel, it is the earlier Beckett of *Murphy* and *Watt*, where the message of ultimate futility is presented in terms of humour and irony. Like Murphy, this novel is set in a London that sounds more like Dublin or Belfast. In fact, *Knock* belongs to an Irish tradition that runs from Charles Lever and Samuel Lover, down through Joyce, Beckett and Donleavy. (One of its central humourous devices – the formal and elegant tone of the postman's conversation – seems to derive from Beckett via Donleavy's *A Singular Man*.) Any resemblance to other writers is due to a similarity of vision rather than deliberate imitation.

The Irish novelist of whom I was most strongly reminded was one that Allen Harbinson has never read – Joyce Cary. And this is because what Allen Harbinson is saying in *Knock* is fundamentally what Cary is saying in *The Horse's Mouth* and other novels of the Gulley Jimson series. The painter Gulley Jimson also lives in a London slum, surrounded by people whose views are restricted by poverty and hardship; their values, insofar as they have any, are totally materialistic. This kind of thing produced in T. S. Eliot the despair that led to *The Waste Land*; Joyce's phantasmagoric Nighttown scene in Ulysses expresses the same outraged sense of rejection. But Cary's Gulley Jimson, another religious visionary, is free of neurotic disgust. Sitting on a tram between an old lady stinking of cabbage water and an old man with a boil on his nose, he reflects on Blake's line: 'Everything that lives is holy; life delights in life…' Jimson feels no disgust because he is untouched by their material values, as an adult is untouched by the squabbles of children.

Allen Harbinson's postman is no visionary artist; yet in his own cheerful, compassionate way, he also lives on another level. He is capable of being unfaithful to his wife, gambling with the rent money, getting drunk on duty, and knocking down a disagreeable child with his canvas bag. But there is one 'human' trait of which he is completely free: malice, or spitefulness. He likes his fellow human beings, and looks upon them with a kindly – if satirical – eye. Even the relationship with his wife – in which there is no element of understanding – is basically affectionate. He wonders idly why he feels no desire for his nubile teenage daughter, and concludes that the answer lies in 'hormones'; the truth is that crude desire is a dehumanisation of its object, and he is too aware of the human reality to treat anybody as an object.

The portrait that emerges is complex and strangely real. In his own eyes, the postman is anything but a saint, and he is capable of fierce bouts of self-disgust (one of which leads directly to his death). Other people recognise the gentleness and compassion that underlie the faults. He would probably be bewildered by the affection he inspires. The transition from the weeping girl at the beginning to the postman's own Rabelaisian stream of consciousness is startling; but as the novel goes on, we begin to see that this device is part of the novelist's basic intention. He is showing us life through the postman's eyes and, at the same time, making us aware of this life as a reality in itself.

When I started to read *Knock* I found myself wishing that the author had employed the same straightforward techniques that Roger Martin du Gard used in his novel *The Postman* (which is one of my old favourites). But within a dozen pages I found that I was totally absorbed in Allen Harbinson's world, and wholly convinced by his method of presentation. Du Gard's novel is objective, and it *stays* on that level. Allen Harbinson begins subjectively, sticking to one point of view, and then gradually expands the reader's awareness until he is moving on two levels: seeing the world through the postman's eyes, and also experiencing it as a separate reality. It is a remarkable *tour de force* and, like all good novels, leaves the feeling that it could have been written in no other way.

I have no idea where Allen Harbinson will go next; but after reading his three novels, I must admit to a consuming curiosity.

Colin Wilson
Gorran Haven, Cornwall
1975

Revelation

W.A.Harbinson

Without warning, after a night of terrifying disturbance, an event
of unparalleled significance occurred to shake the foundations of
civilisation.
It was an event so magnificent, so extraordinary, that it would
alter forever the political structure and the spiritual beliefs of
Western society.
Bringing, ultimately,
the peace that passes all understanding…

'An extraordinary combination of love story, occult, horror and
science fiction… an electrifying read.'
  -*Bookbuyer*

'It's a great idea and Harbinson makes it work wonderfully. A
book with a difference that teases the imagination with its
ingenuity.'
  -*Sunday Tribune*

'It has the lot – love, horror, science fiction, political and
religious intrigue involving the major religions and world
powers, and an extraordinary story of the resurrection of a man
hailed by those religions as the saviour of the world.'
  -*Bookseller*

All at Sea
on the Ghost Ship

W.A.Harbinson

In the year 2001 the son of bestselling novelist and biographer
W.A.Harbinson offered his father a free trip as the sole
passenger on a container ship that would sail from Shanghai to
Haifa, with many other ports in between. Once on board the ship,
Harbinson found that he was the only white face in a crew
composed solely of Indian officers and Chinese seamen. He also
realised that while he had previously sailed on passenger liners,
he was 'all at sea' when it came to a working ship.

All at Sea on the Ghost Ship is Harbinson's account of his
unpredictable, always fascinating voyage. Rich in feeling, acute
in observation, and often very funny, *All at Sea on the Ghost
Ship* is a book to give us hope and make us smile. It is also an
intriguing, rare glimpse into the mind of a writer.

The Writing Game
Recollections of an Occasional Bestselling Author

W.A.Harbinson

The Writing Game is an autobiographical account of the life and times of a professional writer who has managed to survive the minefield of publishing for over thirty years.

Unlike most books on the subject, *The Writing Game* does not try to tell you how to write, or even how to get published. Instead, it focuses with gimlet-eyed clarity on the ups and downs of a unique, always unpredictable business.

On the one hand, a compelling look at a life lived on the edge, under the constant threat of failure, both artistic and financial, on the other, an unusually frank self-portrait enlivened with colourful snapshots of editors, fellow authors and show business celebrities, *The Writing Game* succeeds, as few other books have done, in showing how one professional, uncelebrated writer has managed to stay afloat in the stormy waters of conglomerate publishing.

Here, for the first time, a working author tells it like it really is.

Projekt UFO
The Case For Man-Made Flying Saucers

W.A.Harbinson

W.A.Harbinson's groundbreaking non-fiction work, *Projekt UFO: The Case for Man-Made Flying Saucers*, was widely regarded as one of the most detailed and level-headed books ever published on this controversial subject. It was also considered by many to offer the definitive explanation for a mystery that had haunted the western world for the past sixty years. Now, at last, this revelatory book about 'the world's most fearsome secret' is available to a worldwide readership. *This new edition contains updated material written especially for it by the author.*

Into the World of Might Be

W.A.Harbinson

Two astronauts, a man and a woman, are taking part in a scientific experiment designed to gauge the effects of prolonged isolation and weightlessness on the human body. At first everything runs smoothly, but then things start going wrong. First, the Skylab inexplicably malfunctions, then the astronauts have magical, fearful experiences. But are their experiences real or imagined? Is the Skylab haunted or not? Or are both of them simply going mad?

Into the World of Might Be is a tour de force of prose writing, an astonishingly vivid evocation of the bewildering 'new reality' of quantum physics, alternate or parallel universes, black holes and the mysteries of Time. Uniquely combining hard scientific facts with a philosophical, metaphysical and, at times, deeply religious work of fiction, this could well be the ultimate short text for the New Age… for a new generation. Read it and take wing.

More information on books by W.A.Harbinson can be found at:

www.waharbinson.eu.com

Made in the USA
Middletown, DE
09 April 2022